GW01003336

WHAT'S DEAD PUSSYKAT

Sam Stone

First published in the United Kingdom in 2014 by
Telos Publishing Ltd
5A Church Road, Shortlands, Bromley BR2 0HP, UK

www.telos.co.uk

Telos Publishing Ltd values feedback.
Please e-mail us with any comments you may have
about this book to: feedback@telos.co.uk

ISBN: 978-1-84583-098-4

British Library Cataloguing in Publication Data.
A catalogue record for this book is available from the
British Library.

The author would like to assert that Edward Brewster was not harmed in the making of this book.

Prologue

New York, 1855

It was dark in the chapel when Father Michael came out of the vestry. He was a young man, though wise for his years, with soft blond hair that had a slight curl. His face was angelic, beautiful some would say, and he believed in God and goodness with unwavering faith.

'Father Thomas?' His voice echoed around the eves, unanswered in the hollow, empty space.

Father Michael took a pocket watch out of his long black cassock and peered at the movement. It was 7.30 pm. Mass was barely over, yet everyone, including Father Thomas, was gone. Even the candles, normally fully lit at this time, were all extinguished. He glanced at the windows: it was uncommonly dark outside too.

'Strange,' Father Michael murmured.

The emptiness made him feel nervous, though he couldn't explain why. Perhaps there had been some problem and the congregation had exited, forgetting that he was even there?

But no. Father Thomas would never forget him. Father Thomas was always watching him like a hawk.

Father Thomas was Michael's constant conscience.

Michael briefly recalled the day he had arrived at the church. Young, impressionable, Father Michael had known he was handsome too, and had used his looks and charisma to help ingratiate himself with the parishioners. God had given him what he had in order to use it for his good, after all.

'We've had your sort here before,' Father Thomas had pointed out. 'Best not to be too friendly – particularly with the women. It can lead to all kinds of misunderstandings.'

'I'm here to do God's work,' Michael had said. His angelic blue eyes were benign, but he hadn't appreciated Father Thomas's assumption that he was here to do anything other than his calling dictated. He was loyal and dedicated, and above all believed in God and heaven. Nothing would shake him from that.

'Just see that your desires remain that way,' Father Thomas had said, and the man hadn't let up since.

Always judging. Always accusing him of doing something that he wouldn't even dream of. And those watery, white-filmed eyes looked at him as though they could see right through him: right into his soul. Michael felt guilty most of the time, even though he knew he had done nothing wrong and never would; but it also made him more determined to prove Thomas wrong.

'Father Michael?' a female voice said, and Michael turned to see someone sat in the darkest corner of the church, some distance from the altar.

He frowned, wondering how he had missed her earlier.

'Yes my child?' he said automatically. 'Do you need confession?'

He stepped toward her, wondering who she was. For she surely knew him.

'Lucia,' she said, as though she were reading his mind.

The name meant nothing. Involuntarily Michael shook his head.

'We haven't met,' she explained. Her voice was cultured. English. It was clear she wasn't a local.

'How can I help you?' Father Michael asked.

'Come closer,' Lucia said.

'Let me light the candles. Then we can talk,' suggested Michael.

'No!' Lucia said. 'I don't want you to see me.'

'My child, anything you tell me will be kept in the strictest confidence ...'

Lucia bowed her head. Michael's eyes had adjusted enough to the dark that he could tell she was wearing a veil. She was perhaps in mourning then. One curl of long, strawberry blonde hair fell over her shoulder and peeked out beyond the veil.

'My husband is dead,' she said, again speaking as though she knew where his thoughts lay.

'I'm sorry for your loss,' Michael said. 'I'm sure he has transcended to a greater plane.'

'He was faithless, Father. Like all men. A faithless and untrustworthy animal who thought only of his own pleasure.'

The automatic responses failed Michael. He was, after all, also a man, but one with conviction at least.

A bat flew across the eves, and Michael glanced upwards, grateful for the distraction.

'Faithless,' Lucia said again.

Michael looked back at the bench. Lucia was not there. She now stood beside the altar, a good 20 feet distant.

'What is faith anyway, but a belief in something that cannot be proven? A loyalty based on lies.'

'That's a different issue altogether, Lucia,' Michael said.

The bat flew over the altar. Lucia didn't acknowledge it.

'I came here because of you,' she said.

A shiver ran up Michael's spine. He was suddenly afraid, as though all of the judgemental comments and accusations that Thomas had made might one day be borne out. Was this a test then? Had this mysterious woman been sent to tempt him, as the Lord Jesus had been tempted in the desert?

'You're as beautiful as an angel,' she continued. 'A man of great faith, so they tell me ...'

'Who told you?'

'There are whispers that your faith cannot be shaken.'

'I love God. And no other,' Michael said, and he noted how she flinched when he said the name of the Almighty.

'This church has long been abandoned,' Lucia said. 'Why do you serve here? Why do you every day play out this rhythm of ritual?'

Michael frowned. 'God's house is never abandoned.'

Lucia was silent, and although Michael could not see her face, he somehow knew that she was playing with him.

'You have lost your conviction. I understand that,' he said. 'Maybe I can help you return to God's light?'

'I have not lost my faith, Father. In fact I believe wholeheartedly in good ... and in evil. Look around you. What evil did this to your place of worship? How could man alone desecrate this once hallowed ground?'

Michael's frown deepened. He glanced around at the empty pews, the burnt down candles, the bare altar. The bare altar ... Where were the gold candlesticks? The shining statue of the son of God appeared to have fallen backwards. It was smashed among the choir stalls.

'What evil was done here?' he asked rushing forward.

'And now you *see* it?' Lucia said.

Michael spun around. He saw the leaves and grime covering the floor, the smashed door of the confessional. All of the statuary and paintings that had adorned the chapel were now missing or broken.

'How has this happened? I heard nothing in the vestry!'

A squat gargoyle stood in the corner, out of place inside the building. Its brutish features had once decorated the exterior of the bell tower. He recognised it. How many times had he studied the exterior and interior of this church, seeing all of its beauty and accepting some of the ugliness? He had never liked the gargoyle. It had always appeared to be watching him, wherever he stood. Like Thomas. Spying on him. A surge of resentment filled him, but he immediately quashed it, realising how ungodly and unreasonable this reaction was.

'Father Michael, will you light the candles now?' said Father Thomas from the corner. He unwound himself from the shadows, like a statue coming to life. 'I must have fallen asleep.'

Michael shook his head. The vision of decay was suddenly gone, and so was the mysterious woman.

'What time is it?' Thomas asked.

Michael retrieved his pocket watch once more, like a waking sleepwalker. It was now 10 pm.

'Time we locked the doors,' Michael said. 'Off to bed with you now, Thomas. You've been working too hard of late.'

Thomas smiled slowly. 'What's been happening while I slept?'

'Nothing, Father,' Michael said, but the tremor in his voice belied the confidence with which he tried to speak.

Michael turned to the altar. The gold candlesticks were back in place, the statue of Jesus was upright and undamaged, but as Father Thomas moved into his line of vision, all he saw was the hideous gargoyle. A thick, squat mass with a bulky brow and mean, cold eyes.

'Something did happen,' Thomas said. 'You are upset, Michael. You seem … afraid.'

The bat weaved around the arches above them. Michael didn't look up; instead he stared at Thomas. He couldn't shake the sight of the gargoyle, although when he looked directly at him, Thomas appeared as he always had – a priest who had grown bitter with age.

'Father Michael?' said Lucia. She stood next to him now. The church he knew faded again and Thomas reverted to the gargoyle, frozen beside a shattered pew.

Lucia took his hand. Michael allowed it.

'Faithless male,' she chuckled, but when he tried to pull away, he found his hand stuck in her vice–like grip. 'Look.'

The church fell into rapid decay. This time Michael saw the fall of the statue of Jesus. He heard the crash as its head smashed against the woodwork. Vines were now growing through the shattered stained-glass windows; and, as Lucia pulled him toward the open doorway, he took in the disintegrated steps at the front of the church, now covered with moss and plant life, as though nature was clawing back the space that had once been taken by the building.

'Demon!' he roared, and pulled back on her hand, even though his arm ached right to the shoulder.

'Yes,' said Lucia. 'We *all* are.'

The Thomas-gargoyle moved again with a sound of stone on rock, and suddenly the church was filled with bats. They flew overhead, weaved in and out of the unstable arches, hung from the remnants of the beams.

'Father Michael …' Thomas's voice said. 'Should we light the candles …? I think I fell asleep …'

'Let go of me …' Michael gasped.

'Faithless lover … why did you choose to worship in this godforsaken chapel?' said Lucia.

'I don't know you …' Michael said. 'God is my strength. Yea though I walk through the valley of the shadow of death …'

'Stop that!' Lucia pinched his hand. His fingers were going numb. She raised his hand to her face.

'I will fear no …'

'Father Michael …' Thomas said. 'Should we light the candles?'

Suddenly Michael's hand was released. He glanced down as the blood began to flow back into his tingling fingers. He saw that his wrist was scratched, as though Lucia had clawed him roughly with her nails.

He glanced around the chapel … normal again, except for the gargoyle that was now knelt in front of the altar.

'Father Thomas?' Michael said. His heart was

pounding in fear, his mind juddering on the point of insanity, playing tricks on him in this nightmare that had suddenly become reality.

'Men like you come and go here,' the gargoyle rasped. 'Always attract the wrong sorts ...'

'Father ... help me!'

'Too late. You have her mark now. They won't leave you alone ... not until they've drained you of every last drop ...'

'What's happening Thomas?'

'You lost your faith,' the gargoyle replied.

'No!'

Overhead the bats began to fly. Michael looked upwards and knew there was no going back.

1

New York, Autumn 1865

I lit the stick of dynamite and threw it into the pile of packaging straw. The straw caught almost immediately and I ran toward the window and onto the iron fire-escape. Outside, a rope ladder dangled almost out of reach. I heard Pepper on my heels and flung myself at the ladder. Catching hold of it I began to climb.

'Pull her up!' yelled Pepper as he hung on a few rungs below me. Then the explosions started, and the devastation we had created was far below us.

The warehouse went up in flames as moments later I hurried to the top and onto the tin deck of Martin Crewe's airship. Pepper scrambled over the rail just as the next stick of dynamite exploded below us.

'Gargoyles again?' asked Martin.

'Yes,' said Pepper as he jumped down onto the deck.

'Nasty little creatures,' I said.

'So what *are* these things exactly?' Pepper asked.

'I've been giving the matter much thought,' Martin said. 'Look on them as *escapees*. Like escaping prisoners ... only these little fellers escaped from somewhere else ...'

I wasn't likely to let this one go unexplained, but I had the feeling that Martin was doing his usual playing for time thing, as though he hadn't quite worked out the answer but was on the brink of doing so.

'Escaped from where, exactly?' Pepper asked. He was never as patient as I was with Martin.

'A hell dimension, I expect. But I'm not really sure which one.'

I shrugged. Martin's revelation that there might be more than one hell came as no surprise to me. We had slowly been unravelling the many facets of the *darkness* and its continuing stranglehold on our city, and our world. We were doing our best to hold some of it back, but the work had become bigger than us in the past few months and we couldn't understand why. It was almost as if that negative energy that had almost consumed humanity in the form of zombies[1] was now lurking once more like a thick miasma around us. Something had changed. We just didn't know what. And, furthermore, it was attracting more and more unusual creatures to the city.

'Like an army forming,' said Pepper, as though reading my thoughts.

'Yes,' said Martin.

'And are these things really escapees or did someone deliberately leave the cell door open to distract us?' I asked.

The airship was now way above New York, and I looked down over the buildings. I could still see the fire

---

[1] See *Zombies at Tiffany's.*

consuming the warehouse, and it briefly crossed my mind that the owner of the building would probably be very upset when he returned to find his artefacts destroyed. But art dealers were the worst for bringing in demons in various forms, because ancient stone, art and pottery often carried a residue of their history and were like magnets for evil. I don't know why … they just were.

We were so far above the ground that the world below us appeared unreal. I began to feel that familiar vertigo that accompanied our flights within the ship when we were high up.

'Here,' said Pepper.

I turned to see him holding out a third mask attached to the air tank from which both he and Martin were already breathing. It was something Martin had devised from an idea in his deceased father's notebook: an air tank originally intended for use underwater – which had seemed a radical notion in itself – had now been converted for use at high altitude. His best ideas came when we hit a problem that affected our ability to work well. Lack of oxygen often did.

'You're going green,' Pepper pointed out.

I took the mask and breathed in. Pure oxygen rushed into my lungs and I felt a faint giddiness, but my head soon cleared and my lungs began to feel less tight. Even though the airship was now way above the tallest buildings in the city – some of them were as tall as five storeys – we were now able to cope. My ears popped and I opened my mouth to clear them.

We passed over Manhattan and travelled over the East River.

Once away from the city, Martin dropped the airship lower and we no longer needed the oxygen. We removed the masks, and the tank was stowed into a small cupboard beneath the craft's main control panel. I watched as Martin connected it inside to a filter that replaced the air we had used from the atmosphere outside. I didn't understand it completely but I knew that the filtration system took normal air and purified it until it was neat oxygen.

Martin was particular about ensuring everything was always topped up, charged or replaced once used. He knew that one day we might very well rely on these things to save our lives.

'Take the helm for me Kat, will you?' Martin said. 'I have to go below and feed the furnace.'

I took point at the helm and gripped the wheel in the way he had shown me. We continued over the East River, and by the time Martin returned we were traversing Long Island.

I was enjoying myself as usual. I could see the steam pouring from the two exhausts that were attached one either side of the ship, and Martin smelled of coal but his hands were clean and his clothing impeccable. He was dressed, as my mother often pointed out, like a gunslinger, with his holsters and guns and the peculiar tool belt that always hung over his narrow hips. Of course the broad-brimmed leather hat added to the effect. His personal style made me smile, because I knew it was practical more than anything else. All he lacked were leather chaps covering his breeches.

Martin left me in charge of the helm as he went below once more. We had only a short journey that day, but Martin was always preparing for a longer flight – perhaps even for the day when New York would no longer be salvageable – and the airship was now double the size of the original design. It was big enough to carry several people and provisions easily across the ocean.

I saw the storage warehouse ahead. This was the place where Martin now kept the airship for safe keeping when not in use, along with all of his gadgets and weapons. He also lived there.

As I turned toward the warehouse, Pepper came up to the helm and stood beside me. We had avoided being alone too much recently, but I wasn't sure whether it was me or him who was creating this strange, uncomfortable silence between us. I had the feeling that Pepper wanted to say something. It loomed there in what had once been comfortable companionship. It had all changed the first time we boarded the airship and returned home from New Orleans, leaving the Pollitt Plantation, my brother Henry and his wife Maggie to a hopefully more appropriate future.[2] We had solved a mystery there, and quickly gone on to new ones, as was our want, or maybe bad luck, whichever way you looked at it. I, however, knew I was addicted to the excitement of our world, and demon slaying was in my blood. It was the worst form of addiction. I imagined that even those who chased the proverbial dragon in the opium dens of Chinatown couldn't feel the rush that saving humans from the darkness gave me. Adrenaline, Martin called it. A natural drug that rushes through your veins and makes you react in moments of crisis; dealing with the pressure by taking your fear and turning it into this wonderfully powerful feeling. At such times it would

---

[2] See *Kat on a Hot Tin Airship*.

be easy to convince yourself that you were superhuman. Even though I made a point of never becoming complacent. Never letting myself believe I was invincible. I was human, after all. And these monsters we fought were anything but.

'Kat?' Pepper said. His voice was almost a sigh. It snapped me from my musings even as I thought I must have imagined he had spoken.

His arm went around my waist. I didn't tense. I waited to see what would happen as adrenaline coursed through my veins: only this time it wasn't because I was in danger. I was feeling something new as Pepper, encouraged because I had allowed his touch, moved closer. I could smell his musky aftershave. I liked it. His breath was sweet on my neck. His other arm came around me and I felt ... safe. Pepper was a foot taller than me, but somehow his physique felt right as he nuzzled my neck. And my coiffure, which had become ruffled from the early fight, now tumbled loose as Pepper pressed his face against it.

'I love you,' he said.

I didn't stiffen, but I became still. What did this mean?

I could feel the silence again as though he waited for me to respond. I didn't know what to say, so I turned in his arms to face him.

It was dark as we floated toward the warehouse. And Martin had purposely dimmed all lighting on board. He did not wish us to be observed. Especially so obviously returning to his base. It would have been dangerous, and our enemies were many.

'Pepper?' I said.

I looked into his eyes in the gloom. The moon reflected in the pale blue. I wasn't sure what my response to his words should be, or even if I shared his feelings. I had known for some time now that looking at him pleased me. That his company made me happy in a way that I didn't quite understand. That sometimes, when our hands accidentally touched, I experienced the strangest tingle that began inside my stomach and stretched to parts of me that a lady has no business thinking about. There was this same familiar feeling now. His fingers burnt through the fabric of my clothes, and my heart was racing – but it was a pleasant, not laboured, experience. I tried to analyse it, the rational me forcing its way into the scene when really the emotional reaction was all that should count.

Pepper bent his head toward me as I looked up at him, and I felt for the first time his lips pressing on mine. His mouth was soft and the pressure was reserved and shy.

Not knowing what to do, I let him kiss me. I felt the tingle spread through my mouth. My lips parted, I tilted my head and Pepper took this as a sign to kiss me more. It was nice. Warm. Exciting. My heart beat faster. His tongue slipped into my mouth.

'Ahem!'

We broke apart, and the disappointment I felt at this interruption must have been evident on my face. Martin looked at us both sternly. I felt like a naughty child who has been discovered with her hand in the cookie jar. It wasn't a nice feeling, but the lingering sensation of Pepper's lips was.

I felt Pepper's fingers link in mine, and that leap occurred somewhere inside me. My heart, or my stomach, or both. I couldn't quite be sure what this emotion meant.

'Forgive the intrusion,' Martin said, 'but we are

about to crash into the roof of my warehouse.'

I dropped Pepper's hand and span back to the helm, turning the wheel sharply. The airship veered to one side, narrowly avoiding the collision. Then Martin pushed me aside gently and took over. He manoeuvred the airship carefully, directly into the open roof, and landed it precisely in its docking bay.

'It's late,' said Martin.

There was an awkward moment. As though somehow our momentary lapse had offended our friend. Not for the first time I wondered what life he had outside of our adventures. I had Mother and Sally. Pepper had an ageing aunt that he saw frequently, and his work for the newspaper kept him occupied when we weren't rescuing the city from demonic invasions. But what did Martin have, other than his gadgets?

Climbing down the rope ladder over the edge of the airship I found myself glancing around the warehouse. *Of course.* This *was* Martin's life, and we were a part of it. But was this all there was to it?

'See you both tomorrow,' Martin said.

'Martin ... nothing ...' Pepper began.

The silence was filled with the unfinished sentence ... *nothing has changed.* But it had, and so the words could not be spoken.

I left the men alone as I went into the dressing room and changed my clothing. I pulled my evening dress back on over my breeches. With my hair newly tidied, I looked every bit the respectable lady who was just returning from the theatre.

When I was finished I thought I saw a small shadow passing by the window outside. It was a cat. For a moment I imagined it was my cat, Holly. But I quickly dismissed this thought, as I knew she would be at home with Mother and Sally.

At the warehouse door, Pepper took my hand again. I knew it was right: as though his hand should always be in mine. We walked out into the night in search of a Hansom cab.

Martin didn't say goodnight.

2

Saint Michael's Church,
Autumn 1865

'Why here?' asked Pepper.

Martin, Pepper and I stood before the derelict church of Saint Michael, long abandoned by Rome, just on the outskirts of Queens. The new, modern church building was but a few short blocks away, with a thriving community, while this structure had been left to rot.

'Unusual to see a church building left in such disrepair,' I said.

'This is indeed an abnormal place,' Martin explained. 'Which is why I brought you here in the daytime.'

I tried to wait patiently for Martin's reveal, but the pause was too long. 'Spit it out. What are we looking for?'

Martin smiled. 'You are always looking for an adventure, aren't you Kat?'

'You bet.'

Pepper strode up to the entrance. His leg injury,

acquired in the Civil War some years back, had slowly improved with the constant exercise of our exploits and he no longer needed his walking stick. Even so, he always carried it, his fingers wrapped tightly around the silver cat's head handle. There was a very useful blade hidden inside the stick. A blade that time and again had been used to end the unnatural life of one demon or another: Pepper never left home without it.

The metal gates that had once barred the church were now corroded and had long since been breached. They lay discarded in the path that led to the church steps. Pepper stepped over them and Martin and I followed.

At the main door we stared into the hollow, abandoned shell. The building had been defiled and desecrated. I heard the scurry of rats in the back, and the awful smell of the grave wafted through the open door, as though the bodies from the churchyard had been disinterred and laid out inside to finish their decomposition. I covered my nose, then followed Pepper inside. Martin brought up the rear.

There was still a feeling of reverence, and I sensed that we should walk carefully and talk quietly. Overhead the sudden flutter of wings drew my attention. I glanced up. Light slanted in through the breached roof; the once perfect stained glass windows were all broken. Around us the remaining pews were upturned as though vandals had been inside and had done this just for the thrill of it.

'The relic has been removed,' Pepper said, squatting down to examine the underside of the altar.

'Relic?' I asked.

'Yes – there is always a religious relic inside a catholic altar. Usually a piece of bone from the body of a saint … Probably this Saint Michael …'

'Sounds a bit … perverse,' I said.

'That's religion for you,' Pepper shrugged. 'Anyway, it means that this is no longer considered sacred.'

'So why are we here, Martin?' I asked again.

Martin was silent as he studied the eves above. A pigeon broke away from one of the rotting beams as though something had frightened it, flew around the arches for a minute, then came to rest on the opposite side of the church.

'It would help if we knew what we were looking for?' Pepper commented, but Martin remained quiet and continued to squint upwards.

I shrugged and turned to study the chapel. Past the altar the vestry door was hanging loosely on its hinges. A small statue stood by the door. It was a beautiful figure of a priest. He had an angelic face, not unlike Pepper in looks. Even the hair, which the sculptor had captured perfectly, as though it were flopping in the wind, reminded me of my colleague, and I imagined that the eyes, too, would have been blue if the statue were painted.

'Look at that …' I said.

I walked over to the statue, admired it at close quarters.

'I'm no expert on churches,' I said, having long ago abandoned the regular Sunday trips to the local parish that Mother still took with Sally, 'but they don't usually have statues of modern priests in them, do they?'

Pepper scrutinised the idol. 'It's very realistic.'

I reached out a hand to touch the face of the statue.

'Don't touch it!' warned Martin, snapping out of his trance-like silence. 'Don't touch anything.'

'It would help if we knew what was going on,' I said. I was starting to become irritated with Martin's lack of explanations, when it had been his idea to come to the church.

'All right,' he said. 'There's a tavern nearby. We'll go in there and get some refreshment. Then I will tell you what I know. It would be inadvisable to say anything in here. But for now – just take in everything you see here – and remember it.'

I turned around and began my trek across the grime–covered floor, looking from side to side across the broken or upended pews. A man-sized idol of Jesus was smashed behind the altar. I studied it and noted that the once-painted blood-stained wounds still looked like fresh blood. I looked back to the statue of the priest near the vestry. The sight of it intrigued and concerned me.

'Ouch,' said Pepper behind me.

'What is it?' I asked.

'Nothing, just a scratch.'

'Let me see it,' I said.

Pepper held up his wrist and I saw a thin groove that had barely broken the skin on the back on his hand.

'A splash of whisky on that to sterilise it ...' suggested Martin.

We walked out of the church.

Across the road, a black cat ran into an alley. I found it reassuring.

Despite the brightness of the day outside, the King George's tavern was gloomy. Martin arranged for a private side room for us, and Pepper quickly cleaned the wound with a shot of whisky. I asked for some tea, while Martin ordered tankards of ale for himself and Pepper.

'A few nights ago one of my contacts told me I might like to investigate the church,' stated Martin.

'Why?' asked Pepper.

'He said that he knew I was interested in unusual stories and strange events. The church was abandoned about 20 years ago when they had an infestation of bats. All the normal efforts to rid the place of them failed, and the parishioners began to get sick. Normally robust females became wan; children failed to thrive, and there were reports of devoted husbands straying. Some said statues moved and came alive after dark. There were so many dark and terrifying occurrences that attendance fell. After a while, Rome felt the position here was no longer tenable. So they closed the church. But there were devotees, and so fairly soon afterwards another building was erected a few blocks away. The church flourished again in the area.'

'So Rome just abandoned the other place?' I asked.

'Not completely at first. There were caretakers appointed. But none of them stayed beyond a week. All reported having seen beautiful women and gargoyles that came alive.'

'Gargoyles?' said Pepper. 'So this is linked to our current project?'

'I think so,' Martin said. 'But there's more to it. I'm just not sure what. I mean, the gargoyles are one thing, but I can't explain the women that have been seen, or the bat infestation.'

'We should just blow the place up and have done

with it,' I suggested.

'We can't blow up a church, Kat,' said Pepper. 'That would bring the whole of Rome down on us.'

'But it is for a good cause,' I pointed out. 'And surely it's deconsecrated now?'

Martin smiled. 'Don't ever change Kat. I wish it was as simple as that, though. We know gargoyles don't like fire, but what about these mysterious women? For all we know fire might be the element that's needed to release them from the church.'

'What do you mean?' I asked.

'It was once a holy place. Perhaps they are bound to it. Trapped. Even though the place has been desecrated, there are elements that go into making a building holy. And this one was once blessed. You can't undo that kind of magic.'

Pepper sipped his ale. I knew well the expression he wore. He was thinking the problem through. Mulling over what we should do, with careful deliberation. He glanced at me. A shy smile played on his lips. We hadn't kissed since the time on the airship, and we had deliberately avoided being alone together. His eyes appeared bluer than usual that day, and the pale blond hair that was normally military neat had been left to grow longer. It now fell into his eyes in a very endearing way. I fought the urge to push it aside.

What is wrong with me? I thought.

I sat back, placing my hands under my legs to keep myself still.

'Your tea is going cold,' Martin pointed out.

My hands were trembling when I picked up the china teacup and took a sip. I looked at Martin to avoid staring at Pepper. He didn't have the same glow in his face as Pepper, and I couldn't understand why. It was peculiar that I should suddenly become so intrigued by a friend and colleague who had been nothing more than that to me for several years.

'... things change,' Martin was saying. 'I don't know if destroying the church would be good or bad. It just feels like a very dangerous idea.'

'There must be someone we could talk to about this directly?' Pepper said. 'A priest at the new church, maybe?'

'I'd already thought of that. But my source says none of the current priests were there at the time.'

'I vote we take a trip to the new church anyway ...' I said. 'There may be someone in the congregation that knows something.'

'It couldn't hurt to take a look,' Pepper said.

We finished our drinks and left the tavern. Turning left, we walked three blocks until we discovered the new church. This one was called the church of Saint Michael and Saint Frances. We followed Pepper inside. Pepper and Martin genuflected and bowed to the altar, then the three of us took a seat in a pew at the back. We were on a scouting mission first and foremost. We wanted to observe the community and its priests.

I watched an old woman in widow's black light a candle and kneel at the altar to pray. A young priest went into one door in the confessional box and was soon joined on the other side by a middle-aged man with mutton chop whiskers. A mother with a small baby sat down in a pew to pray. But as the child began to cry, she gathered her up and hurried out of the church. The wails of the child echoed in the high ceiling for a little while longer and then died out to leave a reverent peace.

At that moment a man, probably in his early fifties, staggered into the church. As he passed by our pews, I could smell the liquor on him.

'Farder Thomas!' he slurred. 'I wanna see Farder Thomas Jones ...'

The vestry door opened and a middle–aged priest came out. He was ordinary-looking, with a serious face that made me believe he was a man of devout faith. 'Paddy, please respect the peace and devotion of others ...'

'Farder Simon ... I need to see Farder Thomas ...'

'You know that isn't possible, Paddy ...'

'But I need to tell him what I saw ...'

Father Simon led the intoxicated man away toward the Lady chapel. I stood, slipped past Martin as he remained seated on the pew beside me, and followed the man and priest.

The Lady chapel was much smaller than the main chapel. It was little more than a side room that held a small figure of the Virgin Mary behind an altar. Two distinctive gold candlesticks stood on the altar. They were around three feet tall, with a base and a stem that was wider than my arm. On top of each candleholder was a lit broad white candle. The priest sat Paddy down in the far corner and began to talk quietly to him, but as I stood beside the door unobserved, I could make out most of their muted conversation.

'Father Thomas is sick. You know that ...' said Father Simon.

'I worked there da longest ...' Paddy said. 'I saw dem. And it ruined me, Farder ...'

'You need to pray this darkness out of your soul,' Father Simon said. 'It's the only way forward. When was your last confession?'

'I confess to God all the time, Farder ... He don't listen ...'

'The Almighty always listens, Paddy ...'

'Not to me ... Dey touched me ... I became *faithless*, Farder.'

Paddy's words became gibberish and he began to sob uncontrollably.

The priest finally gave Paddy a blessing, and I moved away from the door and back toward Pepper and Martin, who were already making their way back out of the chapel. We all thought as one sometimes ... We needed to follow Paddy and find out what he knew. Somehow I was sure that the Father Thomas had had mentioned was somehow connected to the other church.

I joined Pepper and Martin outside.

'I will stay and try to find out more about Father Thomas,' I said.

Pepper nodded. 'Okay. I'll call for you later at your house – there's some trouble we have to deal with on Broadway. One of the theatres is claiming to have a ghost.'

'Standard stuff, then,' said Martin. 'Pepper, you stick to Paddy. I will go to the planning offices and try to find out more about the history of Saint Michael's.'

We each went our separate ways.

'Ma'am ...' said Paddy, drunkenly doffing his hat as he passed me. I watched Pepper latch onto the man as Martin hailed a Hansom cab and I went back inside to talk to Father Simon.

'I shall be out again this evening, Mother,' I said,

drawing on a pair of black gloves and a long black overcoat over a grey satin day dress.

Mother was intelligent enough to know that the best way of dealing with her wayward daughter was to turn a blind eye, which she did most of the time. She was tolerant of Pepper's presence in our home. She chose to think of us as innocent friends. And, since the events at the Pollitt Plantation had revealed new aspects of my personality to her, she now knew something of my exploits. After all, we three friends, with the help of the city's cats, had turned back an army of undead, destroyed an ancient demon that was haunting a family, and systematically taken care of a large number of demons in various forms.

'Be careful,' Mother said.

'Aw, you're not going out again!' called Sally, who was eavesdropping outside the parlour door.

Sally opened the door, and Holly the cat bounced in with her and ran around my legs in excitement. The cat had grown a little and was no longer a kitten, but she still remained alert and sprightly and I was always grateful that she lived with us, because I knew she would be there to protect my mother and sister when I wasn't.

'It's not fair!' Sally said, throwing herself down on the couch. 'I want to go to the theatre. Why can't I go too?'

Mother glanced at me. She had noted my odd choice of clothing and already worked out that I would not be going to the theatre that night. She made no comment, however.

'Sally,' Mother said firmly. 'Kat is much older than you. You are barely 13. When you are an adult you may do as you please – within reason.'

'Don't wait up for me,' I said. Then I bent down to stroke Holly's silken black fur.

At that moment there was a knock on the door. I left the parlour with Holly at my heels and Sally's complaints ringing in my ears, but as I opened the door I was surprised to find Pepper there. Often we set off to our meetings alone to reduce the amount of time that Mother saw us together, but then I remembered that he had said he would call for me.

'I need to speak to you,' he said.

'Couldn't it wait until we were …?' I glanced at the parlour door. It was still open, and judging by the silence inside, both Mother and Sally were listening in.

I took Pepper's hand and led him into the dining room. Then I closed the door, leaving Holly on the other side. What was up with that cat? Recently she had been clinging to my heels whenever I was home.

'Okay, what did you find out …?'

As I closed the door and turned to look at Pepper, I was overcome with an overwhelming urge to kiss him, and I had no control over the compulsion. I threw myself into his arms and found an immediate response to my kisses. It was an animalistic, insane magnetism, that was stronger in essence than it had previously been. Pepper *smelt* different. It was as though a burst of light had surged from his bright blue eyes and penetrated my soul until I had no will of my own. The thought of not being around him induced physical pain.

We kissed until my lips hurt. Then Pepper pulled away. I didn't want him to stop.

'I had to talk to you …'

'Yes … something urgent,' I remembered. Today I had also learnt something that I had to tell Pepper and Martin.

I took a breath and was just about to explain what had happened after he had left the church, but his face was so beautiful and radiant that I promptly forgot. We fell into each other's arms again. It was insane, and very unwise. But I just couldn't help myself, and neither could Pepper. The world around us faded away. We didn't hear the knock at the front door, nor Mother entering with Martin until it was much too late.

'Good heavens!' Mother gasped.

At her feet Holly mewed. I took this sound as another form of criticism that managed to mimic Mother's distain to perfection

'Oh!' said Sally. 'It looks like Kat and Mr Pepper will be getting married.'

And that was how George Pepper and I became engaged. In fact, as Mother assumed that more than kissing had been going on between us, we really had no choice.

I couldn't help but notice Martin's look of complete disappointment in us as he turned and left the house without a word. My heart ached with deep regret, but when I looked at Pepper, none of that mattered anymore.

3

Things changed. The idea of marriage became a complete distraction to both Pepper and me. Despite my initial protestations, Mother insisted on a wedding in Long Island. This was partly because it was far enough away from New York City to avoid the rumours of a quick ceremony, and partly because she had found a unique hotel that was willing to organise the quick wedding. It was a replica of a French Chateau, and Mother loved anything French.

'We will go over there for the weekend to try the food and make the booking,' Mother said. 'And the telegram I received from the manager said that, due to a cancellation, they can fit the wedding in next month. Which would be advisable under the circumstances.'

'Mother, there really is no need for a quick wedding. I think it would be better if we slowed things down a little. Perhaps something next year,' I suggested.

Despite my feelings for Pepper, I was concerned by the rate at which my life was changing. This was too hurried. I wasn't sure I wanted a husband; though if I were to have one, Pepper would probably have still been the choice. We were, after all, very good friends, and it seemed a perfect relationship on which to base a marriage.

'Nonsense. The way you two were together I think it very important we do this soon. And I'd prefer that you have no more of your adventures out alone with him until this is settled.'

Mother couldn't be argued with on this point. The week passed by in the most normal fashion. Normal for Mother and Sally, but very abnormal for me, because Mother forbade me to go out at all with Pepper unless we were chaperoned.

'I've been way too lenient with you,' she said. 'And look where that trust has gotten me.'

'Mother. Nothing happened between Pepper and me ... It was just a little kissing ...'

'I don't call "kissing" nothing, Katherine,' she said, using my full name to show that I really was in trouble. 'Kissing leads to other things.'

She busied herself with arrangements for our trip to Long Island, occasionally wafting ideas for the wedding in my direction. But I knew already that my opinion on this didn't matter at all. Mother was genuinely excited by the prospect. Whether this was because she liked Pepper and thought he would make me happy or because she was actually glad to see her unusual daughter settle down, I wasn't sure. Perhaps it was a combination; but whatever it was, the weekend came round and I found myself being pushed into a carriage and we began our journey to Long Island.

Letters had, of course, been sent to my brother in New Orleans, and we'd had a rapid response from Henry that he and Maggie would be there as soon as the date was finalised.

Despite all of my misgivings, I was being hogtied. A few kisses had cost me my independence, and I wasn't happy about it. Not one bit.

It was strange though. When I was away from Pepper I felt nothing at all above the fondness of our friendship. When I was around him, however, I started to behave like a love-sick teenager. I wondered if love was like this for other people, but really had no–one to talk to about it. As a result, my emotions were all up in the air. One moment I was happy, but at other times I was furious that I was being so bullied into this.

'Damn!' I cursed under my breath as the carriage pulled into the driveway of Chateau Chantal.

So this was the place. It was a nice location, surrounded by its own land, and near to one of the best vineyards in the area. Chateau Chantal even boasted its own wine. The building itself looked very European – although I was basing that on travel cards I had seen rather than personal experience. It was something of a folly, a mock castle, with turrets and a courtyard.

'Really Kat, I do hope you are going to behave when the priest meets us to discuss the ceremony. He is going out of his way to do this for you.'

'What priest?' I asked. My blurred memory was jogged. There was something I needed to remember.

'A local church. A Father Peter. Pepper is Catholic, and even though we aren't, they have agreed to do the service.'

'I can't wait to see my bridesmaid dress,' Sally chipped in. 'I hope it's pink ...'

'Urgh,' I said. I *hated* pink.

'It's going to be peach, dear,' said Mother.

'Urgh,' I murmured. That was almost as bad as pink.

The carriage came to a halt and a keen young man in a bellhop uniform hurried down the steps to help the driver with our luggage.

I gave him a tip.

'My name is Brewster,' he informed. 'Edward Brewster. And if you need anything at all, please don't hesitate to ask.'

I thanked him and followed Mother up the steps and into the hotel.

Pepper and Martin were waiting for us near the reception desk.

'Martin! I'm so pleased to see you!' I said. And I was.

Things had been awkward since the night he had seen Pepper and me in our somewhat frantic embrace. He had become wooden around me, and that casual ,comfortable friendship we had always shared was strained. It didn't help that Mother's stubborn refusal to let me go and see Martin meant that we hadn't had the time alone that I needed to sound him out and smooth things over between us.

'Pepper asked me to be his best man,' Martin said.

'But of course!' I said. 'How on earth could anyone else be?'

At that moment the hotel manager came out in a cloud of strong cologne.

'I'm Mr Benderfass,' he explained. 'Can I offer you drinks in zer parlour so zat you can review our vedding menus?'

We followed Benderfass and his tortured Germanic accent into a welcoming salon filled with comfortable sofas. He was an odd and somewhat lecherous little man, with long straggly hair and an ill-fitting suit that he fussed with as he walked. Within a few moments a young blonde waitress approached, carrying a tray full of champagne flutes. I noted how Benderfass followed the girl around like a puppy vying for attention. The girl however completely ignored him. Instead she went straight up to Pepper and offered him the first glass.

'Could we have some lemonade for Sally?' asked Mother as Sally reached for one of the glasses.

'Mother!' said Sally, and for once I actually had some sympathy for my often difficult younger sister.

'Let her have some, Mrs Lightfoot,' Pepper said. 'It is a celebration.'

Pepper had that glow around him again, and Mother warmed to it. In fact she preened somewhat. It was very peculiar to watch, though it pleased me that she liked him and listened to what he said. It would help, if he were to become her future son-in-law.

'All right. But just half a glass ...'

The parlour door opened and in came Henry and Maggie.

'We thought we'd surprise you,' said Maggie.

Henry threw his arms around me and shook Pepper's hand.

'We'd kind of suspected how you felt about each other. Mother's letter wasn't that much of a surprise.'

'How wonderful!' said Mother. 'This will at least turn into an intimate engagement party! You are staying at the Chateau, aren't you?'

'Yes, of course. We'll be here all weekend with you,' Henry said.

'I've booked rooms for me and Martin also,' said Pepper. 'You see, I knew Henry would be here.'

41

Then, as is every girl's dream, Pepper produced a small box containing a beautiful gold ring with a huge diamond in the centre. It was simple and not fussy, despite the large diamond, but just the kind of ring I would have chosen for myself.

'Martin designed and made it for me,' Pepper said.

I glanced at Martin but he avoided my eyes. Yes. Martin knew just what I liked, and so did Pepper. My two best friends in the world. I felt a pang of concern that this was a moment that truly marked a shift in the equilibrium of our friendship. It worried me, but I threw my arms around them both.

'There's also a matching wedding band,' Martin said. 'For the big day.'

I let Pepper slip the ring on my finger, and then that strange blur in reality happened again, as though I had suddenly stepped into an outlandish and fantastical world. It certainly didn't feel like the world I knew. This whole scenario was like a waking dream, but not necessarily in a good way.

Maggie, Sally and Mother clucked and admired the ring, and Mother didn't frown when Pepper kissed me on the lips.

At that moment though the waitress dropped her tray, spilling champagne over the dark red carpet.

'Stupid girl,' Benderfass scolded. 'You need to keep your mind on zee job.'

'I was!' cried the girl, but she was staring at Pepper again in a way that made us all feel uncomfortable. She looked at him as though, dare I say it, she really, *really*, liked him.

'Let's meet here for dinner,' Henry said, breaking the ice. 'We need to go and change out of these travel clothes and freshen up. Maggie?'

Maggie was smiling at Pepper, and only when Pepper lowered his fierce blue eyes did she finally look away. An expression of confusion crossed her features, then she allowed Henry to take her hand and they left.

Mr Benderfass insisted on taking us on a tour of the hotel as Maggie and Henry retired to their room.

'That's a big bed,' Sally commented. And indeed the four-poster in the bridal suite almost filled the room.

'A connecting bassroom,' Benderfass said, pointing to a door off the room.

'What's a bassroom?' whispered Sally.

Mother sighed. 'A bathroom,' she explained, with an apologetic smile at Mr Benderfass.

I found myself blushing in uncharacteristic embarrassment at the thought that Pepper and I would be sleeping in there together.

We returned to the parlour to try some samples of food from the wedding menu we had chosen earlier.

'How are you bearing up?' Pepper asked me, taking my hand while Mother was distracted choosing flowers for the table arrangements.

'I'm exhausted,' I said.

'I love you,' he told me. 'And I'm so happy we are doing this, even though it's been rather quick.'

'You don't feel ... shotgunned?' I said.

'No. It's what I really want.'

I found myself looking into his lovely eyes again. And yes – the use of the word 'lovely' was uncommon for me when describing Pepper, but it was appropriate at that time.

He kissed me quickly again and I felt a little thrill. His words also reassured me. I didn't want to marry Pepper if he were forced into it. Maybe this was right. Maybe my apprehension was normal. After all, weren't all brides-to-be nervous? But as I pulled away and Mother called my name, drawing me back to the moment, that strange anomaly, the blurring, happened again, and I felt a sharp pang of terror that was anything but normal.

I was suddenly convinced that something was terribly wrong.

Pepper, however, showed no signs of fear or concern as he and Martin began a conversation with the flower girl about their buttonhole carnations.

The flower girl listened intently to Pepper, and when he met her eyes she almost swooned.

I met Martin's gaze over the fainting girl's head as Benderfass rushed in to lead the girl away. His expression was impenetrable. I frowned. Maybe I was turning into one of those jealous girlfriends, but the way the other women were behaving around Pepper was making me nervous, and very suspicious.

'I'm zo zorry. I juss don't know vat is the matter with zeeze girls today!' said Benderfass.

Clearly it wasn't just I who had noticed how oddly they were behaving. Even Sally was being overly friendly toward Pepper, and not quite as rude and outspoken as usual.

Back in our rooms – Mother had insisted on adjoining rooms, and I was certain it was because she was convinced that I would otherwise invite Pepper into mine – I lay down on my bed to relax. I had a headache.

It was as though I had been looking intently into the sun all day. It was peculiar how Pepper's attractiveness had suddenly increased, and I had never noticed before how other women viewed him. I didn't feel jealousy, but I did experience a slight pique, and that apprehension remained.

I closed my eyes and tried to push the world aside: a small nap would surely help to shift the anxiety. But behind my lids all I could see was Pepper's face. I was becoming obsessed with him, and it didn't seem healthy.

The door between the two rooms was open and I could hear Mother snoring. I climbed off the bed and glanced in. Sally, too, had collapsed into a doze; the heat and a small quantity of champagne had been enough for both of them. I returned to my bed again and tried to rest, but all the time unease pushed its way into the corners of my mind. What was wrong with me? Was I going completely insane?

Giving up on sleep, I paced the room. I almost wished that we had brought Holly with us. Stroking her fur and listening to her purr often helped me relax.

I was tense, that was all. Everything was happening too fast. I had to remember, though, that nothing need change. Even married, Pepper and I could remain a team, couldn't we? The three of us would still do what we must to keep the darkness at bay. Nothing *would* change. But despite my determination, I had a feeling that it already had.

I pulled my day dress back on. I needed to speak to Pepper. Confront my fears and gain reassurances that things would remain the same between the three of us. And even though I knew being alone with him was risky, the compulsion to see him somehow cleared the headache and helped me make the decision that I *must* talk to him immediately. Opening the door as quietly as possible, I slipped out of my room and headed down the hallway to Pepper's.

I heard voices, and as I reached the door, I realised it was ajar. I found Pepper in the embrace of the champagne waitress, and the floor tumbled beneath me as surely as if I had taken a step off the roof of the Cast Iron Building!

'Kat?' said Martin behind me.

I shook away the stupid feminine swoon and turned.

'Something's wrong,' I said. 'Pepper and the waitress …'

But even as I said the words, Pepper was pushing the girl aside.

'What on earth has gotten into you?' he demanded. 'I'm engaged! Now please leave …'

'You don't want that skinny girl,' pleaded the waitress. 'You need a curvaceous woman like me …'

'Ursula,' Pepper said firmly. 'Leave, or I may have to talk to Mr Benderfass about your behaviour.'

This sobered the girl up, and she pulled away.

'I thought there was some kind of connection …' Ursula whined.

'No …' said Pepper.

'Don't let him see you,' whispered Martin in my ear. 'Come into my room. We need to talk.'

I followed Martin into the room next door and sat down in the chair beside his bed. I felt shocked. And after all I had seen in the past few years, I had thought nothing could surprise me anymore.

'What on earth is going on?' I asked.

'Pepper has become overwhelmingly attractive to

women ...' Martin explained. 'It's not really his fault, and you can see it is not a mutual thing ...'

'How?'

'I don't know yet, but I'm working on it. What did you learn the other day from Father Simon?'

'Father Simon?' My mind was a blank.

The last few days felt like a strange blur of confusion and uncertainty. It took me a few seconds to focus my mind on the name. Then the memory came flooding back. Of course! I had remained at the Church of Saint Michael and Saint Frances to speak to the priest. How had I completely forgotten it?

'Something very strange is going on,' I said.

'I know,' said Martin. 'For a start, you and Pepper aren't really attracted to each other.'

'Of course we are ...' I paused. Were we or weren't we? Hadn't I wondered over this sudden change in our relationship?

'My goodness, Martin, you're right.' That explained it all, didn't it? 'What are we going to do?'

'We need to weigh up the mystery, find some clues and then resolve it, just like we always do.'

4

'I want to tell you about what I found at the planning office,' Martin said.

I was shaken by how we had been totally distracted by the silliness of the impending wedding, and I voiced my concern to Martin.

'Why didn't you come and see George and me to discuss this? That was a week ago, and based on what I learnt at the church, you're right, there is a puzzle, the pieces of which are slowly coming together.'

'I don't know if you realise this, but you and Pepper haven't exactly been easy to talk to recently. In fact when you are in a room together it is as if no-one else is around.'

I didn't agree that we had been quite that obvious, but there was no point in arguing with Martin's perceptions.

'It's all been very distracting,' I said.

'Of course. And we have to find out why this has happened.'

'Well … you see we have both changed how we feel … and …' I said, thinking of Pepper and lapsing back into that weird fantasy world again.

Martin frowned. 'No. You haven't. Snap out of it, Kat. This isn't you. I believe some force is making you *think* you are in love with Pepper.'

'You mean ... you think we are under some kind of spell?' I said, trying to focus on his words.

'Possibly. But I'm not sure. But let me tell you about the architect, and then we can explore what you know,' said Martin changing the subject.

'Architect?'

'The man who designed the church.'

'Why is that relevant?'

'Buildings are designed for purposes,' Martin explained. 'And in the case of churches they are for worship.'

'I know that,' I said, and it was my turn to frown. 'Don't treat me like I'm stupid, Martin. It's getting very irritating.'

'I'm sorry,' he said. 'But you haven't been quite yourself lately. Normally you're two steps ahead of Pepper and me, but this romance thing has you all ...'

'All what?' I said, starting to drift away again at the thought of my husband-to-be.

'Female ...'

I laughed. I didn't point out the obvious, that I was female. I actually knew what he meant. I wasn't myself at all. Even now, when we were trying to centre our minds on work, I was still wondering if the waitress had left Pepper's room. It was obvious he hadn't been interested, but that didn't mean feminine wiles wouldn't persuade him.

'There you go again,' said Martin. 'Blanking out like you're in another world.'

'I'm sorry. And you're right. I can't seem to keep my mind on what's important.'

'The architect,' said Martin, trying again to help me concentrate, 'was a man by the name of Charles Addams. It wasn't his usual line of interest, though he was an artist of sorts. And something of a philanthropist when it came to the church.'

'Okay, I'm going out on a limb here, but why is this relevant?'

'The design of the church is most unusual.'

Martin opened a small leather case that he had left at the foot of his bed. He pulled a roll of paper free and spread it over the patchwork blanket that covered the bed. I stood up and looked at the plans. It was Saint Michael's church.

Although on the surface the plans looked ordinary, something was off kilter. There was the regular design and shape I recognised from the church I had seen, but there was something unusual in the arches. I ran my eyes over the plans, taking in the vestry, the chapel, the markings for where pews, confessional and altar would be. All those things were as I had witnessed in the building itself. My eyes came back to the design on the arches. A strange swirling pattern covered the eves. It had no particular structural purpose that I could make out though.

'Is that writing?' I asked.

'No,' said Martin. 'It's just an odd pattern ... Wait ...'

He stared at the lines for a moment.

'It looks like writing to me,' I said. 'Like Egyptian ...'

'Yes. You know, Kat, I think you're right. Why didn't I notice it? It is a hieroglyphic language. Though not Egyptian.'

'How do we find out what it means?' I asked.

'I don't know.'

I studied the design again and again, trying to make sense of it, and whenever I thought I was close to some form of understanding, my mind glazed over again and I found myself thinking about Pepper. It was very irritating.

'I feel like I should be able to understand this,' I said. 'It reminds me of something familiar, but whenever I try to recall it, my mind goes elsewhere.'

'It's like I said. You and Pepper have been bewitched.'

I didn't want to believe him, even though I knew it was possible. Deep down, despite my misgivings, I was quite enjoying my new relationship with Pepper.

'I need to go,' I said. 'But I'll think about the plans. It feels like the images are already in my mind. It's only a matter of time before I solve it.'

'That's my girl!' Martin said. 'A good bit of problem-solving is just what you need to bring you back to your senses.'

I left, and as I passed Pepper's door, I noted it was now closed. I pondered knocking on it, but then realised that this might not be such a good idea.

Mother and Sally were rousing just as I returned to the room. I quickly stripped off my day dress, lay on the bed and made a loud yawning sound to show that I was awake. A few minutes later, Mother came in and we began to help each other dress for the evening. As she pulled the tongs from the fire and began to curl my hair, I completely forgot about the church plans, as my mind was filled with the chatter of wedding arrangements.

We went down to dinner, and the restaurant was beautifully laid out with covered chairs, silver cutlery and crystal wine goblets.

Pepper was stood by a large mirror in the restaurant.

'You look wonderful,' he said, and when I looked at him my mind became foggy and happy. I smiled at him and barely noticed Martin's frown.

'I have a new invention to show you both,' Martin said.

'Really?' said Pepper, but he didn't take his eyes off me or pursue the line of questioning that he would normally have taken. Instead he just smiled at me in a love-struck, boyish way that was very endearing.

After dinner the men retired to the smoking room for cigars and brandy and we ladies went to the drawing room to play cards. Once I was separate from Pepper, my mind began to clear once more. I wondered if Martin would discuss with Pepper the problem we were facing and the mystery surrounding Saint Michael's Church, but recalling that Henry was with them, I reasoned that it was unlikely.

As the memory of the church floated behind my eyes, I saw myself once more looking up at the eves as the sound of wings beating in the air drew my attention. It was like a flashback of memory. The dark chapel, the chaos and clutter and the smell of decay came floating back to me through a fog of confusion.

I tried to focus my mind while Sally chattered on about the wedding and the plans for my bouquet and her bridesmaid dress. Her constant talking leaked into the vision. I stood up from the table.

'Kat? What's wrong?' asked Mother.

'Nothing. I'm just a little too warm. I think I will

take a few minutes on the balcony.'

I made my way to the French windows that led outside to the veranda, which fortunately was deserted. I went out and felt the cool evening air against my wine-flushed cheeks. The fog cleared from my mind again and a recently-quelled memory slipped through.

The chapel was dark … No. Gloomy. Shadowed shapes hid in the corners. It had been sunny outside but very little light slanted into the building now, even with the broken windows. My mind's eye focused on the far corner and the statue beside the vestry that appeared to have been captured in mid–movement.

This is Father Michael, *said a whispered voice.*

I looked around. I didn't remember returning there, and Pepper and Martin were not with me as they had been earlier.

The shadows to my left seemed to move.

He's ours now. There's nothing you can do …

I closed my eyes, pushing the dark figures away from my thoughts, as I slowly reached into the pocket in my full skirt. There my hand gripped my laser Remington hand pistol. I was ready for a fight if one was coming.

Laughter echoed through the chapel.

That's no use on us …

'Who are you?' I said.

Laughter. Then the sound of beating wings again. I looked up into the eves and saw, a swarm of bats fly like angry bees across the arched roof. They didn't attack though.

You're of no interest …

I frowned into the dark. A shape, bigger by far than the bats, lurked in the curve of one of the beams. It was watching me.

Something moved to my left. My eyes darted away

*from the ceiling as I turned and, pulling the gun free from
my pocket, pointed it at the new arrival.*

'Should we light the candles ...?'

*I knew immediately that it was Father Thomas. He was
the reason I had come there. He had told me something
important.*

*Light slanted in through the open doorway and
Thomas stood as still as a statue.*

*'We need to get you back,' I said. 'You shouldn't have
followed me.'*

*'I must have fallen asleep,' he said, his voice full of
gravel. He coughed once. A burst of brick dust filled the air.
'There's nothing you can do.'*

'Do about what, Father?' I said.

*'Pepper. They've chosen him. There's nothing you can
do.'*

My eyes snapped open as I felt something brush my
leg. I looked down but could see nothing that could
have caused the sensation. It had felt as though Holly
had been there, watching over me, while I had lapsed
into my daydream.

The sound of music came from the parlour.
Someone was playing the piano inside. It was beautiful
music. Chopin.

I walked to the door and there, seated at the
piano, was a stunningly beautiful woman with long,
strawberry blonde hair that cascaded over her
shoulders as though it were a veil. She wore a tight-
fitting red dress that had a flowing wrap over it. Oddly
she wore the wrap not over her shoulders, but reversed
around her neck, and it tumbled down behind her as
the breeze from the window moved it. This left her

arms and shoulders completely bare. Not terribly appropriate, but no-one in the room seemed to mind. She played the piano with passion and yet her fingers seemed light as they moved effortlessly over the keys.

She glanced at me. Her eyes were pale green or blue, I wasn't sure which at that distance. But the perfect high cheekbones reminded me of the classical beauties that some of the great artists of the Renaissance had painted.

She stopped playing, and I noticed that the men had returned to join Mother, Maggie and Sally. They all erupted into applause.

'Bravo,' said Pepper.

I looked at him, saw that warm, fuzzy glow surrounding his beautiful face, and promptly forgot the memory that had just resurfaced.

After the evening's entertainments, I returned to my room and lay back on my bed. A feeling of *déjà vu* pushed around the corners of my mind, and the headache returned with a vengeance. I was trying to recall something, and the harder I tried, the more my own mind resisted.

As I drifted off to sleep, I recalled Father Thomas's white marble skin. He was supposed to be suffering from forgetfulness, wasn't he? But who was Father Thomas?

I probed at the thought in my half-conscious state like a tongue teasing a loose tooth. I couldn't quite grasp the memory, but I was sure on some level that I knew who Father Thomas was. We had met. I just couldn't recall when or where. And I couldn't recall at all the great secret he had told me, even though I knew it was there. It was like a half-remembered abstract dream that promised some fundamental understanding: a deep philosophy that was perfectly clear when asleep but totally eluded the conscious mind.

As I drifted back into sleep I thought I heard a cat purring on the pillow beside my head.

5

The next day passed in similar fashion. Wedding planning, decisions, discussions. I wandered through the events like a ghost, either pining for George or lost in his eyes. It was hard to concentrate on anything much, though I tried my best.

Martin tried to talk to me several times, but, realising that my mind was increasingly elsewhere, gave up and instead sat in the lounge with a pad and pencil, making notes and sketching plans.

By the evening, I was ready for the meal, and was waiting in the parlour with Mother and Sally. There was a chill in the air, so I offered to fetch Mother's shawl from her room.

As I passed through the reception area, a group of young women were there with small bags of luggage. Among them was the strawberry blonde woman I had seen the night before, playing the piano in the parlour. She smiled at me as I passed.

I paused at the bottom of the stairs and, on the pretext of adjusting my shoe, scrutinised the group as they checked in, with Benderfass looking after them attentively.

'Lucia, I'd like a room overlooking the sea,' one of the women said. She had shoulder-length black hair.

Lucia, the strawberry blonde, nodded. 'Of course, Serena.'

Serena was wearing a long black leather coat, uncharacteristic of the fashion of the time. Beneath the coat I caught a glimpse of tight shiny black breeches. On her feet were a pair of black boots, again of a style with which I was unfamiliar. Maybe Serena was a woman like me, who didn't conform with the conventions of feminine fashion? If so, though, she was bolder and more obvious than me. I preferred to appear as though I was the very model of propriety. It made me less conspicuous and my job of demon slaying easier for my anonymity.

Lucia slipped off her coat, and I noted that she was wearing the same dress from the night before. It was beautiful, and it made her pale skin appear almost translucent. Beside her was a woman in a long black floor-length figure-hugging gown, with a very low V neckline that showed off her *décolletage* to what some might feel was a disgraceful degree.

'Here is your key, Mortice,' said Lucia. I noticed that Mortice, like Lucia and Serena, had unusually pale skin but very red lips.

I studied the other women. One had dark skin and appeared to be of foreign extraction. The others referred to her as Natasha, and she was dressed in a gold kaftan. When Natasha walked, she seemed to be so light-footed that she appeared to float. Another wore a long white flowing empire-line dress. Her brunette locks were slightly unkempt and she seemed on the edge of confusion all the time.

'Where's moi spike …?' she said, trying to open

her carpet bag. She had an unusual accent. It was clearly British, but not as clipped as Lucia's was.

'Mortice, take care of Priscilla, will you?' Lucia said. 'She's looking for her "spike" again ...'

Mortice glided over, took Priscilla's hands and led her off to the side, talking intently to her.

Another of the women was a little more mature than the others, but no less beautiful. Her name was Marion and she wore her blonde hair swept up in a neat bun with a black hat, slightly off centre. Her lips were so red that they looked as if they had been painted with fresh blood. She also carried an instrument case, for what I realised must be a cello.

So, they are musicians, I mused.

Saria was the shy one. She spoke in broken English and had deep red hair that was styled over one shoulder. Her skin was pale, but her lips, like Marion's, were red.

'I want a room with a bath,' Saria said to Benderfass as he leered at her over the reception counter.

'I hav just zee room for you,' Benderfass said.

'Camille, I have your beauty cream in my bag,' Marion said as another beautiful blonde woman joined the group. 'Don't forget!' I hadn't noticed this newcomer immediately, because she had been at the door tipping the doorman for carrying in her bag, which was much larger than any of the other women's. She was wearing a long black coat over a black dress that seemed even less appropriate than the clothing the others wore. It was sheer. As she moved, I was certain that I could see her breasts beneath it.

I finished fiddling with my shoe and stood aside as Benderfass came out from behind the reception desk and began to lead the women upstairs to their rooms.

'Vill you be staying long?' he asked.

'A night or two, perhaps longer,' said Marion.

'I want my spike,' said Priscilla again.

'We left it at home, don't you remember? It wouldn't be appropriate to let you swing that thing around here ...' said Lucia, taking her hand. They both passed me.

'You!' said Priscilla suddenly, staring into my eyes as though she were some madwoman newly escaped from Bedlam. 'You're in the way ...'

'Oh. Excuse me,' I said, moving aside.

Lucia smiled at me. 'She has ... problems.' Then she pulled Priscilla past me and they hurried upstairs after Benderfass.

Mortice was the last to go by. 'You have lovely skin,' she said to me, and for some reason it didn't sound like a compliment at all.

As the women left the reception, I stood for a moment longer at the bottom of the stairs. What a surreal experience they had been! Though I couldn't for the life of me understand why, they all seemed completely out of place at Chateau Chantal.

In the dining room, we were placed on a round table with Henry on one side on me, and Pepper on the other..

It was wonderful to see Henry and Maggie. They appeared to be very happy, and I knew that they should have no further issues in their marriage now that the demon had been exorcised from Pollitt Mansion.

'How is your dear mother?' asked Mother.

'She's doing much better, thank you. Especially with the new baby on the way.' Maggie patted her stomach. We were all delighted for them, and the news had been a welcome relief from wedding talk.

'Big Daddy's doing better, too,' Maggie continued. 'He needed a period of adjustment in his new *combined* state. But he's a good man and has overcome many obstacles.'

'I'm sure the *Houngan* is helping,' Martin said.

'Very much so. We don't know what we'd do without Isaac,' Maggie said.

'What's everyone talking about?' asked Sally.

'Nothing,' said Mother, and she promptly changed the subject back to the wedding.

'Let's count this as your official engagement party,' Mother said. 'Tonight, surrounded by the only people we really need.'

Martin raised a toast to us all, and then the sentimental speeches began. It was all rather embarrassing. By the end of the night, though, I was beginning to feel more like my normal self. I didn't know if I was just 'calming down', as Mother would have put it, but I was no longer seeing a hazy glow around Pepper, and I was less frantic about being in his company and having his attention. He also appeared to be the normal him. Though he still smiled as me with a loving expression in his eyes and held my hand whenever he thought Mother wasn't looking.

6

I jerked awake as the sound of flapping wings echoed once more in my ears. I imagined I was back in the church with the bats above me, but then realised that I was still at Chateau Chantal. The hotel room was in total darkness. It was still full night.

I peered into the shadows. A shape rushed across the room, and I slipped my hand under my pillow to search for my gun. It wasn't there. I had completely failed to place it in the familiar spot. What was wrong with me?

I reached toward the oil lamp at the side of the bed, but couldn't find the matches to light it. It was then I decided to run for the door and the gas-lit corridor outside. There I could rouse Pepper and Martin, who would undoubtedly have weapons to hand.

I slid from the bed, but as I hurried toward the door, something struck me from behind. Long claws dug into my shoulder through my nightgown. I gasped aloud, then stifled my cries. The last thing I wanted to do was alert Mother. If she or Sally came into the room then they would most certainly become the target for whatever demon was there.

I had almost reached the door when the creature caught hold of me around the waist and I was thrown hard against the wardrobe. The resounding thump and the loud grunt I gave as the wind was knocked out of my lungs were loud enough to wake the dead, but not Mother fortunately. I could hear her loud snoring through the door connecting our rooms, which was slightly ajar.

The demon grabbed me once more from behind as I tried to crawl to the door leading to the corridor. I elbowed it in what I hoped was the solar plexus and heard a satisfying gasp. The thing fell away. My shoulder stung and my lungs ached, but I managed to pull myself back toward the door. As I turned the key and yanked it open, light from the hallway burst inwards, and the shape of my attacker dissolved into shadow as though I had been fighting a nightmare and not a real entity.

Now that I could see the lamp and the matches, I edged back inside the room, lit the lamp and looked into all of the corners. A bat burst out of an air vent on the wall, flew around the room, then disappeared into the corridor.

I then remembered the church of Saint Michael. Bats. Lots of bats.

The voice of the woman in the shadows came back to me. I had heard those tones again more recently, but where?

I looked around the room. The struggle had upturned a chair. I placed the lamp down on the dresser, straightened the chair, then closed the door leading to the corridor.

So the thing had gone. But where?

In a sudden panic I rushed to the connecting door and peered into the dark at Sally and Mother. All appeared well; they were both sleeping soundly, and the shadows weren't moving in any abnormal way.

I closed the door and reached for my robe. This was indeed very strange. Perhaps it was gargoyles, claiming revenge for their brothers whom we had ruthlessly despatched in the fire we'd created at the art dealer's warehouse? Or maybe it was some other entity whose wrath we had incurred? We were making enemies faster than friends these days. And what on earth was the matter with me anyway?

'Completely forgot my gun ...' I said under my breath, as though chiding myself aloud would make any difference.

I went to the wardrobe and checked out the damage. Fortunately the furniture was unbroken, though I was sure I would be sporting more than a few bruises in the morning.

I opened the wardrobe and pulled out a brown carpet bag with a gold clasp and two short leather handles. I opened it and took a look inside. Without knowing what had attacked me, it was difficult to know which weapon would be effective. My Perkins-Armley purse pistol was a favourite. It shot silver – and diamond-tipped darts from the barrel these days, as it had become one of Martin's many evolving gadgets. There was also the Remington laser pistol, which was fully powered up, thanks to the incorporation of Martin's clever invention of a sun-charging battery. My hand crossbow was fully automatic and could be useful in a fight too. The only trouble with this was that using it inside often resulted in damaged walls if my aim was off or my opponent moved too quickly. That was the thing with demons: they were all different. All had distinctive skills and speeds and needed killing in different ways.

Picking up the day dress I'd worn earlier, I quickly dressed. Something was going on in this hotel, and I was going to find out what it was. Stowing various weapons inside the big pockets that I had previously adapted to conceal them, and placing a sharp gold-plated dagger in the scabbard hidden inside my boot, I cursed myself for not having my more practical clothing – namely my breeches – with me. But there was no point crying over spilt milk – I would just have to make do with the feminine clothing I'd brought instead. Though again I wondered at my own stupidity. The female brain could indeed be very irritating when it became engrossed with romance. It had weakened me.

But never again.

By the time I had dressed and kitted myself out, I realised that I was finally back. Whatever fugue had been clouding my brain was now lifted. I had to go and see Pepper and Martin. I had to tell them what I knew about the church. Somehow I had a feeling that the information was crucial to our survival.

The corridor was deserted. With my weapons in place I was far more confident than I had been in a long time. As I passed the windows facing out onto a courtyard below, I saw Benderfass sneaking around in his nightshirt, a tall candle clutched in his hand. I wondered what he was up to, and so paused to watch as he stopped below one of the windows. Opposite were the rooms of the hotel staff. Benderfass picked up something from the ground and threw it up at one of the windows. I soon realised it was a small stone. He picked up another stone and repeated the process until the window opened and Ursula, the wayward champagne waitress who had propositioned Pepper, looked out onto the courtyard.

'Who is it? What do you want?' she said in a loud whisper.

Benderfass began to sing a romantic ditty – terribly off key.

Within moments, other windows, including those of the guests, began to open. There was much shouting for silence, and Benderfass eventually slinked off, having failed on his obvious mission to seduce one of the help and instead roused the whole hotel from its slumber.

'What's going on?' cried a rotund female as she looked out from one of the windows. She was wearing her yellowy blonde hair in two braids and seemed to be carrying a trident. The room she was in lit up behind her as Benderfass returned.

'Where have you been?' she yelled.

I realised that the woman must be his wife. Through the windows I saw her slap him around the head and chase him around the room with the trident. 'You've been singing to that girl again!'

'Not me! Not me!' he denied.

'Yes you have!'

'Silence when you shout at me!' Benderfass said.

I shook my head and left them to it.

Now that the hotel was awakened, it would be far more difficult for me to look around. Even so, I knocked on Pepper's door.

It took him rather a long time to answer, and when he did I noticed he looked flushed and decidedly guilty. I also realised that my earlier attraction to him had completely disappeared. He held out his arms to me.

'Darling,' he said.

'Stop that,' I answered, slapping his hands away. 'I was just attacked in my room.'

'Oh my god! What was it?'

'I don't know. It was dark. But there was a bat, and I suddenly recalled that I hadn't spoken to you about what I learnt at the church.'

Pepper looked blank. Then he smiled, charisma oozing from his lovely face ... Yes. It was glowing again, and I began to feel confused once more. The blue eyes seemed bluer, the blond hair fairer. I closed my eyes.

'Please don't,' I said.

'Don't what, pussy Kat?'

'Don't turn on the charm like that. It just *isn't* you.'

Pepper sank down onto his bed. 'You're right. It isn't. And why the hell did I call you "pussy Kat"?'

'It's not the only strange thing that's happening in the hotel ... We need to speak to Martin. Has he shown you the church designs?'

It turned out that Martin hadn't had an opportunity to talk to Pepper alone, so I filled him in, while keeping my eyes averted. Looking into those bright blue eyes would have been the end of me.

After I'd finished my explanation we went to the room next door, and a few moments later Martin was showing Pepper the plans for Saint Michael's church.

'You see it is some sort of language ...' I said.

'But I have no idea how to decipher it,' explained Martin.

'Decipher?' said Pepper. 'What's the matter with you two. It's as clear as day. This is a spell. A protective spell. And it's guarding a lair.'

'Lair? For what? Gargoyles?' I said.

'No, Kat. Vampires. This is a very ancient spell.'

'But how do you understand it?' asked Martin.

Pepper was surprised by the question. 'How? I don't know. It just seems *clear* to me.'

In the lamplight, Pepper's eyes pulsed. A throb of darkness ignited in the back of his eyes. I stepped back, horrified by what I could see.

'You've been touched by the darkness!'

And then I remembered where I had seen that same effect before.

'Pepper, what happened when you followed the Irish man, Paddy, from Saint Michael and Saint Frances church?' asked Martin.

Pepper's eyes clouded over. The dark swirl faded and he seemed to be coming out of some kind of trance.

'What happened? Nothing. I followed him, like we agreed.'

'Yes. But where did he go?'

Pepper looked confused.

'I followed him ...'

7

King George's Tavern.
One Week Earlier.

Paddy staggered down the street and turned back toward the King George's Tavern that Pepper, Martin and I had been in earlier. Pepper followed behind, keeping his distance like the trained investigator he was. As Paddy entered the tavern, Pepper followed.

Paddy dug into his pockets, fishing out coins, which he counted in the palm of his hand. He swayed up to the bar, but it was soon evident to Pepper that he had failed to come up with enough money for a tankard of ale.

The barman frowned as Paddy counted his money out onto the ale-stained top.

'Thas s'all I have. Take it or leave it ...' Paddy slurred.

'I'll leave it,' said the barman.

'I don't mind spotting you for that,' Pepper said, eventually. He nodded to the barman, who quickly pulled two tankards and set them on the bar.

'Thas mighty fine of you,' said Paddy, taking the

tankard. 'You're a gent and no mistake.' He swigged from the tankard, spilling a large amount down his chin and over the front of his shirt.

'You seem upset,' Pepper said. 'I hate to see a man upset. Woman trouble, is it?'

Paddy laughed, but it had a nervous, edgy quality. He glanced around the bar as though afraid to be overheard, then dropped his voice in an unsuccessful attempt at whispering.

'If only t'were that simple. It's not *one* woman. It's many. Sure, dey won't leave me be.'

Pepper laughed then too – though he was taken aback by Paddy's claim.

'You might need to confess,' he joked. 'Impure thoughts.'

Paddy frowned. 'Confession ain't no good for no-one. It can't save a soul that's been stolen. Nuttin' can.'

'What do you mean?' Pepper asked.

'Demons. Dat's what dey are. Dey suck der life right out of a you, taking your manhood wid it.'

'That's women all right,' Pepper said. 'I generally try to keep out of their way. Women have always been a big problem for me.'

Paddy nodded his head, then stared down at his now empty tankard. 'Dey are a nightmare ...'

'Barman,' Pepper called. He indicated Paddy's empty glass. It was quickly refilled.

'Tanks,' Paddy said.

'So, what's troubling you?' Pepper asked.

'Tings ...' Paddy murmured. He gulped more of the ale. 'Tings inside der church. Can't seem to get 'em from me head. And Farder Simon won't let anyone talk to Farder Thomas. He's der only one that can help.'

'Maybe I can help?' said Pepper, lowering his voice

into a conspiratorial whisper. 'I know there's something in that church, but I need more information.'

Paddy seemed to sober up. 'What do you know?'

'About the ... gargoyles,' Pepper guessed.

'You mean der statues? Dey move all the time ...'

Pepper nodded, then called the barman back to refill Paddy's drink again.

'But dey are just the lost souls. And I'm going dat way. Der's nothing can be done unless I get to speak to Farder Thomas.'

The Irishman began to cry into his beer. 'Me life's over.'

'Come now, things can't be that bad,' said Pepper.

Paddy stopped crying. 'I suppose der's a worse way a man can go ...'

'So ... the gargoyles?' Pepper prompted.

'Dey are chosen ...'

'Chosen?'

'By der women ... beautiful women. Dey eat up your soul.'

'Barman, more ale,' called Pepper.

'He's had enough,' said the barman.

Pepper turned back to Paddy and found him fast asleep across the bar. 'I think you might be right.'

He paid the bar tab.

'Do you know where he lives?' Pepper asked the barman.

'Yeah,' the barman nodded. Then he gave Pepper the address.

With the help of the barman, Pepper managed to get Paddy into a Hansom cab. A few blocks away, he and the driver half carried, half dragged, Paddy to the door of a small boarding house.

Pepper knocked on the door. A few minutes later,

a young girl with wild dark hair answered. Pepper noticed she wasn't wearing shoes, and her dress only reached her ankles. Having worked with me and come to understand it wasn't fair to judge women for being unconventional, he made no comment.

'Ma,' the girl called back into the house. 'It's Paddy – he's in a terrible state again.'

'Are you his daughter?' Pepper asked.

'Oh lord no! He's just a lodger here. Me ma won't be happy when she sees him though. He owes her two weeks' rent.'

The girl led the way, and Pepper helped Paddy inside and up a narrow flight of stairs. The girl opened a door and they placed Paddy on his bed, where he promptly became oblivious to the world.

They closed his door and Pepper followed the girl back downstairs into the kitchen.

'He drinks all the time. He hasn't worked properly now in weeks. Then he comes out with some nonsense that they don't like his blood when he's drunk. I swear he's trying to kill himself.'

The girl's accent was Irish but far softer than Paddy's.

'We should put him out, really,' she said.

'Why don't you?' asked Pepper.

'It ain't the Christian thing to do. And we look after our own, no matter how bad things get.'

'Did you call me?' said a woman coming in from what Pepper realised was the back yard. She was holding a chicken under one arm. 'Ah, a gentleman. You're not looking for a room *here*?'

'No Ma,' said the girl. 'He brought Paddy back.'

The woman let go of the chicken and it fell with a cluck onto the grey flagged floor. Then it proceeded to walk around the kitchen, pecking at invisible crumbs.

'So he's back?' said the woman. 'Stinking drunk again, I assume?'

The woman sat down at the coarse wood kitchen table and mopped her brow with her apron. 'I swear I don't know what to do with that man. Two weeks' rent he owes me. We can't go on like this, I'm already down to my last three chickens.'

'What's wrong with him?' asked Pepper. 'He was talking about the church.'

The woman crossed herself. 'Fearsome, sacrilegious things he says sometimes.'

'Such as?'

'Romy, get the gentleman something to drink,' the woman said, and the young girl hurried to fetch Pepper a tankard of warm ale. 'Please stay and have a drink, it's the least we can do.'

Pepper hoped to learn more, so he took a seat opposite her at the kitchen table.

'Sure, you're a fine looking man,' the woman said. 'I'm Paula, and this is me daughter Romy.'

Paula sat forward and smiled at Pepper in a way that made him feel uncomfortable.

'I used to think Paddy was a fine man,' Paula said. 'But then he just ... lost it. D'you know what I mean?'

'No,' Pepper said. 'But I'm very interested in what Paddy might have said about the church.'

'The church?' Paula said. Her mind seemed vague now. 'Sure, but you're pretty ... such lovely eyes.'

'Paula?' Pepper said. 'Can you tell me *anything* about Paddy's ravings? It might be important.'

'Sure ... He was always talking about women. They started following him around, and at first I could see it, but then it sort of disappeared ... But you, you have that special something. Do you like poetry?'

'No,' said Pepper. 'But I do like hearing stories of strange events.'

He smiled at Paula and saw the reaction to his charm for the first time.

'It started when he agreed to look after the church for Farder Michael,' Paula said.

'Father Michael? Not Father Thomas?'

'Farder Thomas was there too. But Farder Michael was trying to save the church. You know how these priests get. He wanted to do some form of exorcism. All nonsense. A church can't have anything evil in it. It's just all such superstition.'

'So Father Michael brought Paddy in. What did he want Paddy to do?'

'He was just the caretaker. But Father Michael said "Clean this place up, Paddy". And sure, Paddy agreed. He said, "We are going to save Saint Michael's." I think Farder Michael liked the fact the church had the same name as himself. He was a handsome man. *Just* like you …'

Pepper struggled to pull more information from Paula, but as they talked, she became more and more incoherent. It was as though something was confusing her, and the longer she looked at Pepper, the worse it got. Eventually Pepper took his leave, but as he hailed a Hansom cab to take him back home, he found his own mind became blurred and he promptly forgot the whole meeting.

Chateau Chantal, Autumn 1866

'Until now,' said Pepper. 'But I don't know how I could

have forgotten such an unusual thing.'

'As I said to Kat earlier,' Martin said, 'it's as though some form of spell has been cast that is making you more attractive to women. This same spell is corrupting and confusing Kat. She's turned into a typical infatuated female, and is finding it difficult to focus around you.'

'Was,' I said. 'I'm fine now. In fact I can quite honestly say I'm not in love with Pepper at all. And I quite agree with you, Martin. We've been bewitched. But how and when I just don't know.'

'Without stating the obvious,' Martin said, 'the worst of this started in the church.'

Pepper was uncommonly quiet, and I suddenly realised that my declaration of not being in love might have actually hurt his feelings. Particularly if the effects of the magic were still working on him.

'I'm sorry,' I said quickly. 'That lacked tact, especially under the circumstances. But we both know that this romance thing just isn't us.'

'Of course,' Pepper said. 'I was just thinking ...' But somehow I didn't believe him.

I caught Martin's eye, but he merely shrugged.

'Do you remember anything else?' I asked.

'What?' said Pepper.

'Did Paula tell you anything else?'

'Yes,' Martin said. 'Think man. I know that it's difficult, but you have to try to regain your senses.'

'There was one thing. It was when I mentioned the date. The church has been closed for 20 years, right?'

'Yes,' said Martin.

'She said that Father Michael came only ten years ago. That he tried to do something, then completely disappeared. Paddy believes that Father Thomas knows what happened to him.'

'That's right, of course!' I said. 'I spoke to Father Thomas and ...'

At that moment there was a crash outside on the landing. Martin pulled out a semi–automatic pistol and I retrieved my Perkins-Armley from the pocket of my dress. The three of us were prepared for anything when the door opened and Benderfass came in.

'What are you doing here?' asked Martin.

'I vas looking for your friend,' Benderfass said, nodding to Pepper.

'What can I help you with?' Pepper asked.

Benderfass noticed our armed state.

'Vat is going on here? Is this some kind of weird *ménage a trois*?'

'Good heavens no!' said Martin. 'We were acting out a play. A rehearsal to surprise guests at the wedding ...'

I frowned at the use of the word 'wedding' again. Clearly that whole nonsense must now come to an end, but I appreciated Martin's quick thinking.

'Vatever floats your boat. Anyvey, I vant your help,' said Benderfass.

'With what?' asked Pepper.

'You have a strange attractiveness to the female. I vant you to show me how to do it.'

'Do what?' said Pepper.

'Make a voman fall in love with me.'

'Get out of here,' I said. 'You're a married man. For goodness sake!'

I pushed Benderfass out into the corridor as his wife came along looking for him.

'Vot are you doing in that woman's room?' she

cried.

'Nothing! I'm doing nothing! Leave me alone. You're a monster!'

I closed the door on them both and turned to Martin and Pepper. 'Is it me, or is this scenario somewhat farcical?'

Martin raised his eyebrows. 'Surreal. Completely.'

'You were saying about Father Thomas? I didn't know you'd spoken to him,' Pepper said, and I was relieved that he was finally back with us. I hoped this was a sign that the spell, or magic, or whatever it might be, was wearing off on him too. One thing was for sure: he wasn't doing that whole charisma thing anymore, and for that I was thankful. It was very hard to resist.

'Yes. I went to speak to Father Simon …'

A gust of wind blew the door open again.

'What is going on here?' I said.

The strawberry blonde woman called Lucia was stood outside the door.

'Hello,' she said. 'Is George here?'

'George? Oh you mean Pepper?' I said.

'Hi George,' said Lucia. 'The girls and I were wondering if you wanted to come out for a while.'

'Why on earth would he …?' I said.

Then Pepper began to move toward the door. A blush coloured his cheeks.

'Pepper,' I said, 'would you care to explain why this woman thinks you want to go somewhere with her?' No sooner were the words out of my mouth than I realised we had switched right back into being the future husband and wife again.

'I just can't help myself,' said Pepper.

I closed the door in Lucia's face, turning the lock.

'Pepper, until we sort this out, you're not going anywhere. There's something very wrong with that woman and her friends.'

'I don't feel well,' said Pepper, and he sank down onto Martin's bed.

Martin moved closer and examined Pepper. His skin had turned deathly pale, and when I reached out to check his brow I discovered he was marble cold.

'What's wrong with him?' I asked.

Martin glanced at the door. 'I'm not sure. Probably resisting the spell is having a bad effect on him. But strangely you seem fine. I would have thought that the impact would affect you both.'

'I feel ... normal,' I said. 'But then ... I wasn't the focus of this magic. Pepper was.'

'What do you mean?' Martin asked.

Pepper fell into a deep sleep and I asked Martin to stay with him while I went to check on Mother and Sally. There were a lot of strange things going on and I needed to make sure they were both safe.

As I walked back down the corridor to my room, I saw coming toward me the woman in gold who had been checking in earlier with Lucia and her friends.

'I'm Natasha,' she said as she approached.

'I know,' I said. 'I heard your friends say your name.'

'You're a very clever girl.'

She walked toward me in a peculiar jerky motion that made her appear to float above the ground. Her green eyes were hypnotic and glowed gently as though lit from within, and her bronzed skin shone in the gaslight. I could smell a sensual, smoky fragrance on the air. Her mouth opened in a smile, and I saw for the first time her teeth. Perfect except for a single elongated tooth on one side of her mouth. It was enough for me to realise that what I had believed was only a myth, was actually fact. Natasha was a vampire, and so were her friends. And I'd thought that Father Thomas was just some senile old man who was slowly turning to stone. Everything he'd told me suddenly started to make sense. He hadn't been insane at all.

8

The Church of Saint Michael and Saint Frances
One week earlier

As Pepper and Martin left the church of Saint Michael
and Saint Frances to go on their own separate missions,
I returned inside, to see Father Simon preparing the
altar for Mass. Not really sure how I should approach
the priest, I took a seat in the back pew again.

A short time later the church began to fill up with
worshippers, and I felt the moment had been lost.

I sat through the Mass, remaining, I thought,
inconspicuous in my seat as many people went up to
the altar to partake of the sacrament. The prayers
finished and the choir was still singing the final hymn
as the congregation began to disperse. Then the priest
walked past me to the front of the church, followed by
his altar boys.

I was still uncharacteristically at a loss to know
how to approach and ask him about the conversation
he'd had with Paddy – because surely he would just tell
me the same thing he had said to the inebriated
Irishman – when Father Simon appeared at the end of

the pew.

'He wants to see you,' he said.

'Who?' I asked.

'Father Thomas Jones. That's why you're waiting, isn't it?'

I wondered if this were a case of mistaken identity, but thanked my good fortune for the opportunity to gain an insight into what was going on. So I followed the priest to the back of the church toward the vestry. Just as I passed through the door, I glanced back to see if we were being observed. I noticed a woman sat in the front pew. She was dressed in black, with a full veil covering her face. I had the most peculiar feeling that she was watching me.

We exited through the back entrance of the vestry and Father Simon led me to the rectory, which was just a few feet from the church. This, I knew, was where several of the secular priests lived together. Father Simon didn't take me into the house through the front entrance however. Instead he led me around the building and out to the back yard – which was long and wide with neatly cut grass. I noticed a small, flat-roofed building at the end of the yard, partially hidden by a row of tall bushes.

'He hasn't been himself for some time,' Father Simon warned. 'Not these last ten years.'

'I understand,' I said.

The number didn't correlate with the timescale of the closing of the church, which according to Martin had occurred 20 years earlier, not ten. I began to wonder if Father Thomas had even been around at the closure of the other church, or if he were merely some aging priest that Father Simon was entrusted with. Either way I wanted to meet him. There had been something in the urgency of Paddy's voice when he had asked to see Thomas that made me believe this meeting could be important.

'He is … confused most of the time,' Father Simon said. 'But he specifically asked to see you, Miss Lightfoot.'

I blinked. The priest knew my name. This wasn't just some fortunate coincidence after all.

'I see,' I said, and I reached into my coat pocket to feel the reassuring sensation of the cold barrel of my Perkins-Armley pistol.

Father Simon opened the door of the small building, and we entered a vestibule where a middle-aged nurse sat at a desk facing the door.

'This is the lady Father Thomas wished to see,' Father Simon said.

The nurse peered at me over small, round-rimmed spectacles, then nodded. She stood, pulled a key from her pocket and proceeded to unlock the door to a room behind the desk. I could see that she was more than just the old man's nurse; she was also his gaoler.

'He wanders sometimes,' Father Simon said, as though my suddenly blank expression had given away my suspicion. 'He's very old. Ninety-seven next week. We worry that he will get hurt.'

I nodded. Who was I to judge? I didn't, as yet, understand the situation.

The nurse stepped aside, and I looked to Father Simon to lead me into the room, but instead he took a seat on a chair near the door.

'I'll be here if you need me,' he said.

The nurse gave me an impatient look until I walked toward her. Then she pushed open the door and stepped back to let me inside.

The room was dark and musty. Heavy drapes were pulled across the windows, even though it was now getting dark outside. I suspected that the windows were locked too. I looked around to see a single bed, a small wardrobe and a matching dresser. The floor was bare wood, but a rug was placed beside the bed in an attempt to offer some comfort and warmth. There was a chair close to the door.

Despite Father Simon's comment about Thomas's 'wandering', the form sitting on the other side of the room didn't look very capable of moving. In fact he looked as still as stone.

'Father Thomas?' I said, my voice a whisper.

I was greeted by a rasping snore, and I realised the old man was fast asleep. I sat down in the chair by the door and let my eyes adjust to the gloom.

The old man was seated in a cane rocking chair with a thick blanket draped over his legs.

There was a smell in the room that reminded me of death. Thomas didn't have long, I was sure of that.

'Should we light the candles?' he rasped suddenly. 'I must have fallen asleep.'

'I'm sorry to disturb you,' I said. 'Father Simon said you wanted to talk to me.'

'I knew you were there,' he said. His hand came up slowly and he rubbed the sleep from his eyes.

'Would you like me to open the curtains?' I asked.

'No. The light ... damages me.'

'I'm sorry,' I said.

'Why? I don't mind ...' he said.

I couldn't imagine living my life in this gloom all the time, even though I spent most of my time fighting evil at night. I loved to see the daylight and the sun. It reassured me that we were winning the battle against the darkness – even though I knew that the darkness would always be there, trying to break in, trying to shut out any goodness that light represented to me.

The room was stifling hot. I unbuttoned my day coat and slipped my arms from the sleeves. I didn't know what to ask Thomas, so I hoped that he would just talk. Maybe even reveal something about the mystery surrounding the old church.

'Do you get many visitors?' I asked, breaking the long silence.

Thomas's head turned, and I felt him scrutinising me in the dark.

'They've stopped me walking,' he said. 'They keep me locked in here. They believe I am a danger …'

'They are afraid you will injure yourself …'

'Not myself … They feel I will injure others. But I'm not that far gone yet …'

The priest leaned forward, and I sank back into my seat. His eyes glowed with a swirl of darkness that made them appear like deep pits filled with cold fire. His skin was grey and dusty, marked with thin lines that looked like cracks.

'You're …?' I gasped.

'A gargoyle?' he said, but his voice was gentle. I saw him struggle with the evil inside him, and slowly the smoky black flames faded, leaving the pale watery eyes of a very old man.

'Yes …' I said.

'Not quite. But sometimes it takes me, and whatever I do in those moments, I cannot remember afterwards.'

'Blackouts?' I asked.

'If it helps for you to explain them, then yes. But

I'm not insane. I'm not mad. In fact I have all of my mental faculties. Perhaps my mind is even sharper now than it used to be.'

'How?'

'Something has infected me. Changed me.'

I waited. Thomas wheezed as if he were struggling to breathe. His mind may have been strong, but there was no doubt that his body was failing.

'I called you here to tell you a story. Today you went to Saint Michael's.'

'I did,' I said. 'How did you know?'

'They tell me. I sometimes see through their eyes. But they also can see through mine.' Again that black swirl guttered into life in his eyes and flared before vanishing once more.

'Who are *they*?' I asked.

'A black wave of evil swarmed into the chapel just before we closed for the night. They took the form of bats, but that was only a disguise.'

'Gargoyles, disguised as bats?' I asked.

'No. But the two are linked.'

I tried to pull the information out of him in a quick barrage of questions, but Thomas merely shook his head, and his impassive face forced an amused smile at my impatience. I sat back in the chair and gave the appearance he wanted. I was the listener, he the storyteller.

'It was 20 years ago,' Thomas said. 'I was an old man then, but strong and healthy. I had led a careful life and tried to keep in good physical shape for the sake of my demanding parishioners. I had seen many of them married. I had christened their children and grandchildren. Buried more than I cared to recall. This was a thriving community, though, and for the most part we lived without too much loss. I did my best to comfort those that suffered it, too. I was a good priest. Did my duty. But it all changed when *he* arrived.'

Thomas paused, and I waited as he seemed to be collating his thoughts.

'His name was Father Anthony. He was young, impetuous. Totally dedicated to his faith. A true believer in the grace of God. Anthony was an inspiration to us all, and the ladies of the parish liked his youthful beauty, which meant that there was record attendance on the Sundays when he led the service.

'Anthony was so innocent and naive though that his fall from grace was somehow inevitable. I can see that now, and I wish I'd known then how to warn him. How to save him.'

The priest coughed, his trembling hands clamped over his mouth as he spluttered, but what came out of his lungs made me think of the marble dust that might fill the air in a sculptor's studio. His breath smelt of stone, and a chill breeze wafted from his struggling lungs.

There was a jug of water and a glass on a table at the bottom of the bed, and I left my chair to pour him a drink. As I handed him the glass, his cold hands brushed mine. I suppressed the shudder that threatened to ripple up my spine from his stone-cold touch. His skin, already resembling the solid aspect of a marble carving, was as frozen as a corpse's.

The coughing fit ceased and I sat back down, glad of the distance the bed between us gave. Thomas composed himself, and then he spoke.

'Anthony didn't deserve what they did to him,' he said. 'But I get ahead of myself.

'Autumn had just begun to set in when they

arrived. Anthony was from Alaska, and he had been admiring the golden browns the leaves were turning. He greeted the seasons with childlike innocence. That night, he had been admiring the stars outside while I snuffed the candles on the altar. "Ouch", he said. When I asked him what was wrong, he said he had gotten a splinter from the door.

'Then he staggered. I rushed to see what was wrong. He looked pale, shocked. "Are you all right, Anthony?" I asked as I led him back inside and closed the door. He nodded but sank down into one of the pews. A few seconds later he seemed fine again, and I thought that he had suffered just a momentary dizziness. We both soon forgot the incident and carried on snuffing the candles and locking up for the night.

'The next day, something odd occurred at Mass. The ladies had always liked Anthony, but now, suddenly, his preaching brought them to tears and applause in equal measure. They loved him. Really *loved* him. Naturally I became a little concerned. Too many of them remained behind after the service, all asking for his advice, vying for his attention. Anthony was unperturbed by it though. He answered all of their questions, gave out good advice, perfectly as his calling dictated. I watched him like a hawk. He wouldn't have been the first young priest to have had his head turned by excessive attention. But Anthony didn't waver. His faith was solid.

'A few weeks later, his impact on the ladies seemed to lessen. Anthony became distracted though. He began to talk about one woman he had seen in particular. He said her name was Lucia.

'I didn't know who he meant, and I said so. "But you must know, Thomas. She's the widow. The English woman. The one that sits on the back pew at evening Mass."

'I told him to point her out next time she arrived, and he said that he would. "I feel so for her, Thomas. She has no-one in the world. She is an orphan and now is newly widowed too." I looked at him, noting the passion with which he spoke, and I suddenly felt compelled to remind him of the vows he had taken. Anthony became angry with me then, saying I was misunderstanding his concern. But I'd seen more faithful priests than him led astray by a pretty face. In my years at Saint Michael's I'd seen all of them come and go.

'Anthony was called away again. By another demanding female. I watched him go, then I turned to the altar and gave a silent prayer for him. I was truly concerned about the way things were going. There was an atmosphere in the church that hadn't been there before. And Anthony remained a magnet to the young women, even though the effect was less intense than it had been initially.

'That night I took Mass. The church filled with the usual people, but I peered over their heads to the back pew to see if I could recognise the woman of whom Anthony had spoken. I saw a movement, and the black veiled woman he had described joined the congregation. I knew all of the parishioners and their children, but she was completely unfamiliar to me.

'After Mass, I stopped by the pew. I had hoped she would come up to partake of the sacrament, but she hadn't. It was as though she had come to the church merely to observe. "May I help you, my child?" I said. She turned her head and looked at me. I couldn't see through the veil at all; she could have been hopelessly scarred beneath it for all I knew. "I've come to see Father Anthony," she said. She was English, just as he had said – I could at least determine that from her accent. I explained that Anthony was currently in the confessional.

'She stood and brushed past me, and something on her dress, maybe a pin that had been left in the fabric, caught against the back of my hand. I pulled my hand back as though I had been bitten by a serpent. By then, Lucia, if this was she, had passed by me and was moving across the aisle.

'She sat next to the other women who were waiting to give their confessions to Anthony. I walked back up the aisle toward the altar, but when I glanced back I noticed that the confessional row had diminished. The women in front of Lucia had all suddenly changed their minds and left the pew. At that moment, the woman inside the confessional came out. Lucia went inside.

'A chill wind blew the church doors open with an impossible strength. I chided one of the altar boys, whose job it was to secure the doors after Mass. "I closed them, Father. I really did," the boy said. I sent him on his way with a sharp word that warned him about telling lies, particularly in God's house. The boy walked away, head bowed. He looked confused and had such a hurt expression in his eyes that I did have a momentary pause. It wasn't like him to be lax. Maybe I had been too harsh.

'I began to prepare the church for closing as the last remaining worshipers drifted out. I glanced toward the confessional. Lucia was still inside – at least I hadn't seen her come out. It wasn't like Father Anthony to take that long, particularly at the end of the day when we were all beginning to feel tired. After all, we were up at five every morning to prepare for Mass.

'Finally I was alone in the church when the woman barged out of the confessional. The doors flew open again, and a torrent of what I took to be black birds poured inside. "Good Lord!" I said. "What is happening?"

'Lucia threw aside her veil. "I'm no longer widowed," she said.

I thought it a peculiar thing for her to say, but at that moment Father Anthony staggered from the confessional. He looked sick, and I rushed toward him. "Don't touch me, Thomas," he said. "I've lost my faith."

'Anthony fell against the pew, knocking his head. Above me the birds, which I quickly realised were actually bats, flew around and around in the eves. I didn't know it then, but Saint Michael's had become cursed, and so had Anthony and I.'

9

Thomas paused in his tale as though the wind that had rushed into the church had suddenly taken his breath away. He coughed again but refused the offer of more water.

'It doesn't really help,' he said. 'My lungs are turning to stone. And so are my other vital organs.'

'How?' I asked.

'The woman, Lucia. She was a night creature. A soul born from darkness. And she was not alone in the world. She had sisters, and all of them needed to feed.'

Thomas lapsed into the second part of his story.

'Lucia threw back her head and looked at the eves. As the bats swirled, a strange pattern began to reveal itself in the plaster above. "I knew this was the place," she said.

'Anthony had reached the altar by the time the swarm descended on him. He was marked, you see. And Lucia had brought her family to him. Like a mother bird feeding her chicks. She had made Saint Michael's their new nest, and there was nothing we could do to stop her.

'The horde surrounded Anthony, picking him up

clear off the ground! Then, within seconds, they dropped his body, now a drained and dry husk, back down, where he landed hard against the statue of our Lord Jesus Christ. The statue fell, completely dislodged by the impact, and smashed into the pews.

'I'm ashamed to say I ran out through the vestry. I thought the very devil had come inside the church and taken over.'

Thomas stopped, and that swirling darkness glowed inside his eyes once more. 'I was right, of course. The devil had come, or rather sent some of its minions to destroy us. I didn't know then, of course, that their poison was already inside me too.'

I waited for the black light to leave his eyes once more before speaking again. The sight of it took my breath away. I knew what it meant. I also appreciated that Thomas had been fighting his own personal demons for 20 years. His strength had to be admired.

'I returned the next day with the police,' Thomas said. 'Anthony was dead. They assumed that we had been attacked by criminals, and I had been careful what I told them; after all, I didn't want to be placed in an asylum. I had administered enough last rites in those places to understand what went on there.'

'So you decided to close the church?' I asked gently.

'There was no choice. Those things had taken over. You should have seen Anthony. He was completely drained.'

'Of blood?' I asked.

'More than that. He looked like an empty shell – as though he had never lived at all. A broken statue, not a human.'

I reached across the bed and took Thomas's hand

as I heard the pain in his voice. His fingers were like marble, smooth but with grooves representing the lines that a sculptor might copy to provide realism. I pushed aside any feelings of disgust.

'You're kind. A good soul,' he said. He pulled away then, and I sat back in my chair once more.

'We tried to clear the church. We brought in experts to destroy the bats and held exorcisms to clear away the evil. Finally an emissary from Rome, a Cardinal, came to take a look. No sooner had he walked into the chapel than Lucia appeared once more in the shadows. It was daytime, but the light that had been filtering in through the windows suddenly become obscured. Lucia was wearing the veil again. "Who is this?" asked Cardinal Benedict.

'I grabbed the Cardinal by the hand and pulled him outside. "You must stay away from her," I warned. "She is the evil that manifested itself among us."

'Benedict was shocked by my sudden terror, but he was experienced in dealing with these matters. He looked me in the eyes and said, "They've contaminated you, Thomas. We must close the church or you will end up like Anthony." But I knew he was wrong. I was too old and did not have enough life to give them. They would need to feed, though, and I had to make sure that no-one suitable went near the place again. This was the centre of their power, you see? They could feed only in the church. I knew this, because some of their knowledge seeped in my direction.

'We appointed a caretaker. An elderly man. But soon he reported seeing Lucia and other women there. And there were claims that Father Anthony's spirit brought alive the gargoyles. That wasn't true, of course. We had taken care of Anthony's body. It had been burned to ashes, never to be used by this evil. Never to return as one of their moving statues.

'Caretaker after caretaker came and went until finally Paddy was appointed. He was the last one. You saw him outside … talking to Father Simon.'

I nodded, and this time I didn't ask him how he knew. The scratch had taken something from Thomas, but it had also given him an interesting insight. I suddenly remembered that Pepper had been scratched in the church, and I began to feel concerned.

'Cardinal Benedict decided I should no longer be around the parishioners,' Thomas continued. 'I was put out to pasture like an old horse that had served its master well. I was fighting the demon inside me, but I was considered no longer safe to be around the flock. They didn't know what I was capable of, after all. But at first I did have some freedom. I was still treated like a loyal servant of God, out of respect for my long service to the church. That wasn't in question, nor were the loyalty and faith that have since helped me keep the demon at bay. But I cannot answer for those lapses; and it was on one such occasion that I led another of our young faithful servants right into the hands of those creatures.

'His name was Father Michael.'

Thomas relayed the sad tale of Father Michael. A young man who had followed what he thought to be 'the wandering old fool' back to the old church. There the creatures, starved for several years, had hooked onto him.

'It was ironic that the church was named after Saint Michael,' Thomas said. 'That amused Lucia immensely, and they played with him at first. Thomas Made him imagine the church was normal. It was the cruellest thing I had witnessed, and I couldn't help him. The fugue state took me over and over again. I tried to break into the visions they gave him, but Michael wasn't strong enough to fight them. He was arrogant deep down, you see? He believed he was faithful and beyond reproach. But really that was his fatal flaw. They took his faith, and his soul, along with every drop of blood they could drain from his living body, turning him to stone. They love to corrupt those that seem incorruptible.'

I realised I had been holding my breath when my lungs began to protest. I breathed out, then immediately in. The air rushed to my head and I felt a momentary dizziness. I had seen Michael – he was the priest statue!

'It's all so horrible,' I said. 'Thomas, there must be something that can be done to save you, and release the soul and body of Michael?'

Thomas looked at me. The black swirling light was back in his eyes.

'There is a way,' he said. 'But I won't allow *him* to tell you.'

I was looking into the *Darkness*. I knew it, and it was the most terrifying moment of my life. This was the evil we had been fighting as it hid always on the periphery of our vision. Now I saw it face on, and it saw *me*.

My chair crashed to the floor before I even realised that I had leapt up. I backed away. At that moment the nurse opened the door from outside and looked in with Father Simon, a concerned expression on both of their faces.

'Miss Lightfoot, are you all right?' Father Simon said.

'I think we're done here,' I said. I wasn't sure I could take any more. I believed I had looked right into the very soul of the devil.

'Don't trust *him* pussy ... Kat,' said Thomas behind me.

I glanced back at the old man to see that he had fallen asleep once more. If he had been mounted outside of the church I wouldn't have given him more than a cursory glance: he was a gargoyle.

'He hasn't got long,' said Father Simon as he closed the door of Thomas's room. The nurse quickly locked it.

'What is going to happen to his remains?' I asked.

'He's requested cremation. It's not something we generally approve of ... but special permission was given by the Pope himself.'

'It's the only way to be sure,' I said.

'What did he mean by "Don't trust *him*"?' asked Father Simon.

'I don't know,' I said. 'He was just rambling, I guess.'

But I believed I did know. Thomas had warned me not to trust Pepper. It was obvious really.

I wasn't satisfied, so I returned immediately to the church. That was where I had my worst fears confirmed: Pepper had been contaminated.

10

Chateau Chantel,
Autumn 1865

Long, sharp nails swiped the air as I ducked, narrowly avoiding them carving up my face. Natasha crashed into the door of the room opposite. There was a loud protest from within the room, and I hoped for their sake that the occupant wouldn't open the door, as Natasha turned back to face me once more.

Fury flashed through her eyes.

'You are in our way,' she said. Then she flew at me once more.

I threw myself forward into a head roll and, despite the annoying skirt I was wearing, managed to come back up to my feet. My heels snagged briefly on the hem, but I lifted up the skirt and ran full pelt down the corridor. I had to lead the vampire away from the others, then learn how to despatch the creature.

I pushed through the door that led to the staircase down to the lower floors and the reception.

Mortice was waiting for me in the stairwell. I turned and kicked out at her, landing my foot on her midriff. It wasn't enough to displace her, but the tight-fitting black dress she wore tangled in her legs as she tried to grab me. It gave me the perfect opportunity to push past her.

I tried to run, taking the stairs two at a time, but the bulk of my own gown was causing me serious concerns. On the next floor down, I pulled free the weapons from the pockets of the dress and, taking my knife from its sheath in my boot, cut the laces that held my clothing in place. The dress dropped to the floor, leaving me dressed in long black stockings, pantaloons, a white camisole top and a pale blue corset: which meant that I was, in society terms, quite indecent. I tucked my Perkins-Armley into the top of my corset, my knife back into my boot, then continued my flight down the stairs with greater ease.

As I reached the reception area I saw Priscilla. She was still wearing her long Empire-line black dress. I was bizarrely aware that the fabric was so thin that it looked just like a nightgown. She was holding something in her hands. A big metal pole with a sharp spike on the end.

So someone has finally given in and found her weapon, I thought.

I pulled the Perkins-Armley pistol from the top of my corset. Priscilla didn't approach me, however. She merely stared at me across the room. Then someone dropped on top of me from above.

The air was knocked from my lungs – which was getting to be an annoying and painful habit – and the gun went off in my hand. Then I felt a sharp pain as the weapon was yanked from my fingers. My wrist hurt, I could barely breathe, and I was yanked to my feet by my hair. I heaved in lungfuls of air until the pain in my chest eased and my head began to clear.

'This is the reason we haven't eaten yet, sisters,' Lucia was saying. 'But I can't for the life of me understand why the bond with this pathetic female hasn't yet been broken.'

The vampire called Marion came to study me. I was being tightly held between two of the women. One was Serena, who didn't seem too menacing for a vampire. Despite her unusual haircut and shiny black breeches and coat, she was very quiet compared with the rest of them. A little sulky, if the truth be known. The other one holding me was Camille, who was wearing a sheer white nightgown. She was also quiet, but I didn't like the way she leered at my underwear.

'She's very beautiful,' said Marion. 'Maybe he *is* in love with her.'

'Don't be ridiculous,' Saria said. 'Men don't *really* love. We all know that. They are faithless.'

'I'd like to play with her before we kill her ...' Camille said, and the way she emphasised the word 'play' made me think of a cat 'playing' with a mouse.

'We don't need another sister. There are enough of us to feed as it is,' Lucia said.

I struggled, but my shoulders ached from the effort. The women had me in their vice-like grip, and I had no way of pulling free.

'She's pretty,' said Priscilla. 'Loik a kitten. Can I 'ave her? Pretty thing.'

'Too messy,' said Lucia. 'Though I'm sure you'd have fun, Priscilla. We could feed her to the wolves.'

'Where are we going to find wolves around here?' said Serena. 'Besides, she's just a human. And no-one we need concern ourselves with. Let's lock her in the hotel office and go and finish what we came here for.'

As I listened to her talk, I realised that the thing they had 'come for' was Pepper. I couldn't allow them to take him. It wasn't a fitting end for a fearless demon-hunter and a soldier who had survived the worst kind of horror that the civil war could offer.

Serena and Camille began to pull me toward the reception desk.

'It's a pity,' said Camille. 'She would make a beautiful addition to our ranks.'

Realising that Camille's interest in me was far more like that of a man, I decided to try using my feminine charms – not that I had much experience of this. I arched my back and pushed my breasts forward.

'I like you too,' I said, smiling at her with as much charm as I could muster.

'Ooh,' said Camille.

Camille's hand slackened on my wrist for just a second, but it was enough for me to slip free. She tried to grab me again, but as my hand touched hers she jumped back with a scream.

A thin burn appeared across her palm. I slapped at Serena with my now free hand and heard the satisfying fizz as the flesh on her cheek began to burn. I found myself released as her hand came up to her cheek to feel the wound I had inflicted. She didn't cry out, but she looked at me with a wounded expression that was altogether too human.

'And I told them not to kill you,' she said.

'Gold!' said Marion.

It is a common misconception that all demons are allergic or have an aversion to silver. It was one I had believed in and used to my advantage in the past. But not these ladies. They, it seemed, were repelled by gold. It burnt them; although how or why eluded me. But the gold engagement ring was the cause of the damage I had inflicted on them.

I held out my palm and they all backed away. Lucia was the most repelled, and she sank back into their midst as the others surrounded her. This was most interesting to me, because it seemed that they were willing to risk themselves rather than her. They watched me like caged lionesses. Their wistful expressions implied they remembered being free and craved the hunt.

'Get away from me,' I said. 'And you'll leave Pepper alone. He's not for the likes of you.'

I backed toward the stairs, not knowing what I would do, but was sure that I had thwarted them for the time being at least. Then I felt something clink against the heel of my shoe. Without lowering my hand I glanced down and saw my gun on the floor. I bent swiftly and picked it up, replacing it in the front of my corset.

'We can't *leave* him,' Saria said. 'He *belongs* to us. He has Lucia's mark.'

'Be quiet,' Lucia said.

I was halfway up the staircase before I was brave enough to turn my back on them and run the remaining flights.

I was out of breath by the time I reached my floor and knocked loudly on Martin's door. Martin opened it immediately and I fell inside. I would have to trust for now that Lucia and her sisters wouldn't be interested in Sally and Mother. It was clear that it was Pepper they wanted and they had gone after me because they knew I was in the way. But that didn't mean that Martin wasn't in danger, because it was obvious that the women fed on men. How they did that, and indeed why they chose any particular victim, was beyond me at that moment.

'What's happening?' Martin said. 'Are Sally and Mrs Lightfoot okay?'

'I think so,' I said when I had caught my breath. 'One of *them* attacked me as I tried to get back to my room.'

'What happened to your dress?' he asked, and I remembered what I was wearing.

'Damn! This will be difficult to explain to Mother …' I said.

I described what had happened in detail and also filled Martin in on my recollection of my visit with Father Thomas and my return to Saint Michael's.

'Pepper could turn into a gargoyle? Is that what we've been fighting these last few months … the remains of these monsters' meals?' Martin said.

'I'm not sure, but Thomas admitted that the gargoyles and vampires were linked. Unfortunately the demon inside him wouldn't let him tell me how to destroy them.'

'Pussy … Kat …' muttered Pepper.

I watched him turn over on Martin's bed. He appeared to have a fever.

'Funny. That's what Thomas called me too. What's happening to him, Martin?' I said.

'I can't describe it. You need to see for yourself.'

He brought the oil lamp over to the bed, and I took in a sharp breath when I saw the pale skin on Pepper's face and neck. He already appeared to be turning to stone. I felt sick. Sick with worry and horror at the possible fate of my best friend. This was all too much.

'Obviously the injury he received at the church

was from the vampires,' Martin said.

'They marked him.'

'Shame we don't know which of them did it, though,' Martin said.

I barely heard what Martin said as I sat down beside the bed and held Pepper's hand. It was as cold as Father Thomas's had been, but with less rigidity. 'Maybe he will hold out, just like the priest did.'

'Possibly. But according to your account, Thomas was safe only because they thought him too old to pursue. He wasn't a hearty enough meal to feed them all.'

'You'd think at least one of them would ... Wait.'

'What is it?'

'They were protecting her.'

'Who?'

'Lucia,' I said. 'They were protecting Lucia. She's like ... how did Thomas put it "a mother feeding her chicks". That's what he said. Or something like that.'

'Then that means she is their mother,' Martin said.

'No. It can't be. They were all different ages. They call each other "sister" but they don't look related at all. Some of the other women are clearly much older than her. But they *are* like some kind of family. Plus, I remember now ... the other women said Pepper was carrying *her* mark.'

'The women were turned at different ages,' Martin said. 'They are vampires now, Kat. But they began life as human. All mythology about them shows that they are turned and become these things. Before then they would have aged until the time they were taken.'

I pondered this revelation. It was certainly true that they had discussed bringing me into the fold. I told

Martin what Camille had said in that regard.

'But Lucia was concerned about having another mouth to feed.' I explained.

Martin sat down on the bottom of the bed. Pepper turned, releasing my hand, but didn't wake.

'There's something I have read somewhere,' said Martin. 'But it doesn't correlate with what I know about vampires.'

Something bumped against the door. Both Martin and I jumped.

'Pepper,' said Lucia through the door. 'Come out and we'll leave your girlfriend alone. You belong to us.'

Pepper sat up on the bed.

'No you don't,' said Martin. Then he punched Pepper on the chin, knocking him out cold.

Outside the room, Lucia screamed, and the sound was what I imagined a banshee would make when its prey slipped away.

'Get the hell out of here, Lucia. Pepper's not coming,' I said.

'Then we'll come in there and get him,' Lucia said. 'And your other little friend, too.'

I placed my hand against the door. The gold band of my engagement ring began to glow as if it had captured sunlight inside it. From outside Lucia yelped.

'Wow,' said Martin. 'Even through the wood.'

'Never underestimate the power of gold on a girl's finger,' I said, but I didn't feel glib.

'Let's hope the fear of that holds them off until morning,' Martin said.

'Why morning?' I asked.

'Vampires, historically, live only by night. They can't take sunlight.'

'I'm not sure that's true in this case. But I hope

you're right. It will give us some breathing space.'

As the corridor grew quiet again I pulled my hand from the door and returned to my seat next to Pepper. He was sporting a substantial bruise on his jaw, but I was sure that he would forgive Martin for it when he woke and learnt what was happening. For now, though, I wanted him to remain unconscious. It would be far easier to stop those creatures manipulating him that way.

'Maybe we should tie him down?' I said.

'That would make him more vulnerable,' Martin said.

I told Martin to try to get some sleep, and he curled up on the floor by the bed with a pillow. Soon he was snoring, and I sat with my eyes on the door. If gold was poison to them, then my ring was one piece of jewellery I wouldn't be parting with for the time being. I studied my hand, still bemused at the power of the gold. What was it that this metal had that repelled them so much?

Just then a rock hard fist came down on the back of my neck. I fell forward out of the chair, and face first into oblivion.

11

'Kat? Kat?'

I came to with a thumping headache and blurred vision.

'What the …?' I said.

Martin was looking into my face. His brow wrinkled with concern. 'Are you all right?'

'What happened?'

'Best guess, Pepper woke up and knocked you out.'

'What? Why would he do that?'

Martin said nothing. He didn't have to. It was obvious that Lucia had broken through to Pepper's mind and made him attack me. This was a terrible revelation. It meant that despite our friendship she was breaking down his defences.

I dragged myself up into a seated position. I was on the bed. 'How did I …?' My mind was still fuzzy.

'I pulled you up on the bed when I woke and found you. I'm sorry I slept through the whole thing.'

The bedroom door was closed. I pulled my legs over the side of the bed and sat up, but my head hurt so much that I dropped it into my hands.

'That was one hell of a punch,' I said.

While I recovered, Martin explained that he had woken to find me unconscious on the floor, Pepper gone and the door closed behind him.

'I guess he didn't want those things to get in here,' Martin said.

'Which means that he wasn't completely under their spell when he left,' I commented. 'Otherwise, why not hand us over?' The thought heartened me somewhat.

I stood up and tottered precariously on my heeled boots.

'You probably have a concussion,' Martin said.

'No time for that. Martin, lend me some clothes. We are going after him, and we are going to finish those she-devils once and for all.'

'How? We have only the gold ring as a deterrent.'

I pulled the gold-plated dagger from the ankle of my boot. 'I have this too. But something about that knock on my head rearranged my brains enough to realise something else.'

'What?'

'Without Lucia, the others can't feed.'

Martin wasn't sure that my theory was correct. Nor that the small dagger and ring would be sufficient to help us destroy Lucia – because, based on my theory, that was all we needed to do.

'Lucia is the link in all of this, and it should have been obvious to me sooner. If I hadn't been in a state of romance-induced insanity, that is.'

I dressed in some breeches and a shirt that Martin found for me. Then we hurried out of the room to go and find Lucia and her sisters.

We found Benderfass behind the desk in the

reception area. He was looking at his register with some consternation.

'Mr Benderfass? Which room is Lucia in, please?'

'Lucia?' he said. 'I don't know a Lucia.'

'The girls ... they all arrived last night. I saw you ...'

Benderfass went blank. I pulled the register out of his hands, and as I looked down, I realised that half of the rooms in the place were empty. The girls hadn't officially checked in. That was clear. Instead they had used some form of hypnosis on Benderfass to make him give them rooms.

There was no easy way to do this, so Martin and I began our room to room search of the hotel, starting with all of the seemingly empty rooms.

After we had searched several rooms and found no evidence at all of anyone having stayed there, I realised that this might be a waste of time.

'Even so, we have to check everywhere for them,' I said.

But it infuriated me. My patience was running out. All I wanted to do was find Pepper and ensure that he was safe. But to do that we had to continue our search. On my floor I checked in on Mother and Sally, who were, thankfully, oblivious to all of the night's dramas.

'One last unoccupied room and then ...' said Martin, turning the key in the door of 210.

The door opened. A strange smell wafted out into the corridor. Like all of the other rooms, this one was in total darkness. The difference was that someone had also left the curtains closed. Martin was carrying an oil lamp, and it cast a circular beam of light into the room. I saw the shapes of furniture, the bed, a dresser, a wardrobe and a chair – not dissimilar to my own room.

There was a shape on the bed. Someone was sleeping here, but there was no sound coming from them. Martin nudged me and I glanced at him. He indicated that I should draw my gun. We moved over to the bed; the occupant didn't stir.

My heart thumped in my chest as a familiar run of adrenaline pumped through my veins. I was a coiled spring waiting to be released.

With his free hand, Martin pulled back the sheet. He raised the lamp. His uniform was all crumpled, but we could see it was the friendly bellboy, Edward Brewster, who had helped bring in our luggage when we arrived at the hotel.

'They fed on him! That explodes my theory that they can feed only in the chapel,' I said.

'No. His neck is broken. They might have been having a little fun that got out of hand. But see … no scratches, no bites,' Martin said as he examined the body.

'We need to inform the police,' I said. 'Poor Mr Brewster. But at least he won't become a gargoyle.'

'When we've finished our search we'll have to tell Benderfass. But first we had better check the occupied rooms,' Martin said.

He rummaged in his jacket pocket and pulled out some fake identification and a badge that showed him to be an inspector from the New York Police Department.

It was 4 am before we finished checking every room, much to the chagrin of the disgruntled occupants. We roused them, got them to open their doors and made a quick inspection of the interiors, all under the pretext of looking for an escaped convict who had been seen in the area. But for all the effort and time it took, we failed to find Pepper.

'I need to wake Henry and Maggie and arrange for them to take care of Mother and Sally in the morning,' I said. So far we had deliberately avoided Henry's room. I hadn't wanted to panic him and Maggie, but now there was no choice.

Martin went away to hire a carriage to take us back to Manhattan. There was only one other thing that could have happened: the vampires had taken Pepper back to their lair.

I knocked on Henry's door. It was the last room in the hotel to check, but I was pretty certain that the vampires weren't there.

'Who is it?' Henry said through the door. He sounded groggy and tired, which wasn't surprising given the unnatural hour.

'It's me. Kat.'

Henry opened the door and stared out at me.

'You're wearing men's clothing,' he said after a moment.

'Yes. You should have seen me a few hours ago,' I said. 'Can I come in? I need to tell you something.'

He stepped back and I walked inside. The room was dark, but Henry lit a lamp and then closed the door. Maggie was in the double bed in the corner. She didn't stir.

'She sleeps through anything,' Henry said.

'So do Mother and Sally,' I said. 'Oh for a clear conscience.'

'What's the matter? Wedding jitters?'

Henry perched on the edge of the bed as I sat

down in a chair beside him.

'It's far more serious than that.'

I told him of the vampires and their marking of Pepper as their next victim.

'I need to make sure you'll take care of Mother and Sally. Mother will be very upset when she realises I've left the hotel.'

'I should come with you,' Henry said.

'No. I'm used to dealing with these things. Before they messed up my head with romance, I had quite a strong personality.'

'But are you as strong now, Kat? If these things have a hold on Pepper like you say, and your heart is entangled in this with him, then how can you be as formidable as you were? And yes, I know you're strong. I saw it. Thanks to you, I have a marriage now and Maggie's family are free. But I'm afraid for you.'

'I can't risk you too,' I said. 'These things are dangerous to men, Henry. They will eat you alive, and where will Maggie be without you?'

Henry bowed his head. 'This is all wrong. I'm your older brother. I should be protecting you.'

'Life isn't as straightforward as it used to be. In the old days I'd have been glad to have had my brother be there for me. But a lot has happened. I'm not some poor, helpless, naïve female anymore, and I can fight my own battles.'

I left Henry, and he reluctantly let me go when I pointed out that Mother, Sally and Maggie needed him to take care of them and he would help me more by doing that.

I returned to my room, picked up my carpet bag, but left the rest of my things there. My weapons were the only things I needed.

Martin was outside when I finally left the hotel, and true to his word he had acquired a pony and trap.

'Not the quickest way to travel,' he said.

'I bet you wish you had brought the airship,' I said.

'I would have, but I knew your mother would kill me. It's not so far to my warehouse from here though.'

12

Back at the warehouse, Martin insisted on making some last-minute adjustments to our weapons. We had an argument about it. I was very anxious to follow the women and get Pepper back, but I realised that quarrelling was wasting time anyway.

He cranked up his smelting oven and threw clumps of gold into a pot, placing it in the heart of the fire. Then, when it had sufficiently melted, he dipped each of my crossbow arrows into the gold before carefully placing them in a separator tray. We carried the tray onto the airship. At least the cool air up above would help the metal to harden, but Martin still wasn't satisfied that we were properly equipped to take on eight vampires alone, with just a mini crossbow, my gold dagger and an engagement ring for weapons, so he also brought along the Remington 1958 that we had used when the zombies had cornered us in Tiffany's. That was some time before, and Martin had since made modifications to the design.

'For a start,' he explained, 'the cartridge had a problem. Do you remember how it would twist up when it was almost empty, making the last bullets useless?'

He loved to show me his new designs and gadgets, and I realised as he talked that we hadn't spent much time alone recently. I always loved to hear about his new inventions.

'I remember that it almost got us killed once,' I said.

'Well, no more.' He opened the bullet case and pointed to the conveyor. 'It was simple really. This now runs on rails rather than a gun-belt, and so can't twist. I don't know why I didn't think of it sooner. What I really ought to do now is tip the bullets in gold – but unfortunately there isn't time. Hopefully the diamond shards inside will still do significant damage to any foe, even vampires.'

I remembered how the bullets would explode inside the zombies, sending diamond off-cuts out into their bodies like shrapnel. It caused the maximum amount of damage, so his theory was reasonable, even in the case of vampires. It might even be enough to kill them. We just didn't know, because we really hadn't faced them head on yet.

He strapped the pack onto my back and I placed the Remington barrel down in the holster that Martin had made for me some time ago from tanned hide. Now dressed in my own breeches and shirt, with a short, black velvet jacket, I buckled the holster around my waist and thigh. I was beginning to feel more like myself again. It felt like a long time since I had geared up for a fight, even though it had been only a few weeks of distraction that had taken me from regular working mode into a realm of female fantasy.

I helped Martin attach another tank to his own back.

'This is a flame machine that I've been working on,' he explained. 'It throws out fire. More controllable than dynamite.'

'Sounds good,' I said.

'It's pretty volatile,' Martin admitted. 'Full of flammable gas. So I had to double-line the canister to protect it from any outside heat. It works a little bit like gaslight burners, but has more projection due to the valve here.' He pointed to a place on the long nozzle. 'The wider it opens, the faster the gas pours out and burns – throwing the flame further in the process.'

I checked that the gold blade was still in my boot and hung the crossbow onto my belt along with the empty arrow cartridge. The arrows would be loaded just before we landed, if they were ready. If not, then we'd use my regular arrows, hoping that they would at least slow the creatures down a little.

It was almost sunrise by the time Martin released the moorings on the airship and the balloon, freshly filled with gas, began to rise up out of the warehouse.

We arrived above the graveyard of Saint Michael's. Fully equipped with my favourite weapons, I hurried down the rope ladder and ran around the front, while Martin moored the airship. I reached the front steps only moments after landing.

The sun was coming up and I could see two figures standing guard either side of the broken church doorway. One was Father Thomas. The other was the statue we had previously seen inside the church. I suspected this one was Father Michael.

'Thomas?' I said.

'Shall we light the candles, Father Michael?' said

Thomas, his voice like grating rock. 'I must have fallen asleep.'

Father Michael didn't stir. Outside, the statue was no longer a skilful carving of the priest but had become a hideous gargoyle. Its once beautiful face was drooping and elongated, resembling melting wax rather than stone. I put a foot on the lower step. Michael-gargoyle turned its head and stared at me. The eyes blazed into life with that dark, swirling fire. I removed the Remington from its holster and clicked off the safety switch.

'Thomas. Michael. I'm coming up the steps, and I'm going inside. If either of you try to stop me, I will destroy you.'

Michael-gargoyle's mouth opened in a sinister leer. It didn't speak, because it couldn't. It was merely the minion now of the evil we had been fighting. But the leer was a threat in itself. I had a flashing image of being torn apart between the two statues. Yes – gargoyles could send you waking nightmares like that. It was one of their specialties.

'Pussy ... Kat?' said Thomas.

'Yes ...' I said as I began to walk up the steps. 'It's me. Kat Lightfoot. We talked a few weeks ago. Remember?'

Michael-gargoyle began to shift as though its limbs were remembering how to move. It was almost fully turned in my direction.

Martin was following on my heels by then, and he quickly caught up with me as I reached the last step.

'You almost forgot these,' he said, slamming the arrow cartridge into the crossbow on my belt.

'Careful ...' I said as we began to move between the two gargoyles.

At the door of the church, Michael–gargoyle began to swivel quickly. Its mean face twisted into a characteristic sneer – characteristic for gargoyles, that is. It raised its heavy fist, and I lifted the Remington and fired before it could deliver a crippling blow. I didn't think my head could take another knock that night: I was still feeling shaky from the one that Pepper had given me.

Michael-gargoyle hopped back as the bullets buried themselves into its stone bulk, but no real damage was done.

'Kat!' called Martin.

I glanced quickly in his direction to see Father Thomas coming forward. He still had a human aspect, despite the stiff movements his limbs made.

'Shoot him!' said Martin.

'I can't. He's still alive in there!'

Michael-gargoyle was flanking me, trying to block the entrance to the church. This confirmed to me that Pepper must be inside. I didn't want Pepper to turn into one of these things, and so a red mist descended on me. I fired again and again at the approaching creature, pushing it backwards with each shot, and continued until I had managed to force it back into a corner and allow me access to the door.

Martin was struggling with Thomas. The priest had his stone hands clasped onto Martin's shirt. I turned and hit Thomas hard on the temple with the butt of my gun. He staggered. There was a strange flicker as he seemed to lose the gargoyle countenance, and then he slumped into the other corner looking like the very old man he was.

I had no time to check if he was still alive; I turned back to the Michael-gargoyle as it began to approach me again. I continued to fire diamond shard bullets into it, while Martin lit his flame machine. The moment the fire poured out of the nozzle, the Michael-gargoyle cowered back. Gargoyles hated fire. Despite their stone appearance, they were incredibly easy to burn; something that had made no sense to me until recently, when I had realised that they were once human bodies that were being inhabited and manipulated by demons. Martin pushed the gargoyle back by casting an arc of flame before it. It lost its footing and tumbled down the stone steps, cracking into three large pieces at the bottom.

Not dead, but disabled, the creature could now be left while we focused on far more important things. I had to get inside and rescue Pepper. Time was running out, and I realised it could already be too late. I just didn't know.

Martin went in first, curving the flame around the entrance just in case there were other gargoyles waiting inside. The way was clear, however, and we entered the church unaccosted.

Once inside, the flame machine sputtered and died.

'Major flaw. The gas burns out very quickly,' Martin said. 'Something I need to work on.'

With the light from the flame gun extinguished, the church plummeted into darkness. Dawn was upon us, but the sun hadn't quite made it high enough up to light this tomb-like space.

I heard a yell in the dark, and turned the Remington to face that way. Then a swarm of bats dived downwards from the eves, directly at me.

'Don't let them scratch you!' I yelled, conscious that Martin was vulnerable.

I dived to the left, Martin to the right, and the bats poured out through the open door and into the daylight.

Once outside, the bats burst into flame, like hundreds of fireworks, and cartwheeled down to the ground, where they exploded into puffs of ash.

I knew then that the bats were not normal creatures; they were probably some evil conjured up by those ghastly women.

I saw a flash of Lucia's red dress, and then I felt the sheer fabric of Camille's nightgown brush against my hand. It was as though I had accidentally caught myself in a spider's web. The Remington was whisked from my fingers, but the thief didn't get far, because the gun was firmly attached to the metal tank on my back. Instead, the perpetrator was yanked back against me as she tried to flee. I slammed my ringed hand onto her head. Whichever vampire it was, she had long hair, and I was able to twist my fingers into it and hold on, even as she bucked against the pain of the ring burning into her scalp.

Finally the skin and hair, burnt to a crisp, came away from her head, and the creature fled to some murky corner of the church. I was left holding part of her scalp, and a clump of long dark hair with it. I looked at it dispassionately. It was probably Priscilla's, because the hair was too long to be Serena's.

The sun had risen higher in the sky now, and its rays were beginning to filter into the church, but a gloomy mist remained to obscure our view. I was used to being in shadowy places and, as my eyes adjusted, I began to make out shapes in the dark. Over where the altar stood I saw Camille and Mortice. They were holding something. I realised with shock that they had

Martin. He struggled against them, but I remembered their grip well and knew he wouldn't be able to free himself.

I holstered the Remington and pulled the crossbow free. Using the gun was too risky with Martin in the line of fire. All I could hope was that the gold-plated tips would do the job against the vampires.

As if he knew what I was going to do, Martin stopped struggling and fell to his knees. The two women were taken off balance and fell together. They each released Martin and he span away, crawling on all fours toward me. I pressed the load button and fired instantly at the women before they could part. The larger target made it easier to hit at least one mark.

There was a yelp. Mortice jumped away, but Camille fell backwards against the altar. The arrow had hit true. It now protruded from her breastbone, and the skin fizzed, then burnt. A slow fire began in the centre of her chest. It was as though the gold tip was acid to her flesh. She screamed and yelled and thrashed against the altar, then burst into flames, filling the church with more than enough light to see where all of the other vampires hid.

I marked their location in my memory as Camille died. And it wasn't pretty, or quiet. She made as much noise as she could before finally crumpling into a pile of blood-red ashes.

Martin reached me as I span around and sent an arrow careering toward Serena. But she was too damn fast. She did an impossible leap and flew up into the air. A swarm of bats greeted and surrounded her as though they were helping her fly, and ultimately land, onto one of the crossbeams. I sent the next arrow in the direction of Marion. She wasn't as fast as Serena, and the arrow hit her in the shoulder as she tried to flee. She fell behind a stack of upturned pews and began to pummel the ground. In the next moment, one of the other vampires had reached her and yanked the arrow out. I heard the clink as the metal tip hit the ground somewhere in the corner. To my left, Priscilla came rushing at me again. I backhanded her with my free hand, and felt a sharp scratch across the back of it. It felt like a tooth. A sharp, pointed one. Afterwards my hand ached, but I was used to pushing past pain, since this was a common occurrence when you found yourself battling against the creatures of darkness.

The rising sun's rays finally burst through into the nave of the church, and the vampires scurried deeper into the darkest corners – which showed that there was some truth in Martin's assumption that vampires couldn't go out in the daytime. A flurry of bats burst from one corner and drove upwards toward the roof. They disappeared into a cavity in the ceiling that I could barely see.

I could see Martin clearly now. 'Did they hurt you?' I asked.

'No.'

'Are you sure? I can't risk you going gargoyle on me.'

He pulled off his gloves and held up his hands. I examined them, right up to his wrists, but he was unmarked.

'What about you?' he asked.

I waved the scratch before him.

'Looks the same as the one they gave Pepper.'

'I'm not male, though,' I said. 'I doubt that I'm a suitable meal. Besides, I think she caught me by accident rather than intent.'

We both crouched down behind some pews, and I thought I saw Lucia's red dress floating into the light in the far right corner, nearest the door that led to the former vestry. This had been where we had seen the statue of Father Michael originally, and I wondered if the room held particular significance.

'There,' I said, nodding toward the shadow.

'Lucia?' asked Martin.

'I think so. Cover me.'

I ran down the gap that had once been the aisle, brought the crossbow up as I reached the vestry and shot straight into the corner.

Saria fell forward. I had forgotten that she had also been wearing a red dress, and realised my mistake as she died at my feet in a burst of flame – though she went with quiet dignity, unlike Camille.

'Sun's up,' Martin said behind me.

I looked around and found there were no remaining shadows in the church. All of the vampire women had gone.

We hurried into the vestry, but much to my disappointment found the place completely empty. The derelict room was bare, save for a thin rug and some built-in wardrobes with doors hanging off their hinges. We checked inside the wardrobes anyway, but came up blank.

'Where is he?' I said. 'Where is Pepper?'

Frustration and fury gave way to a fracture of emotion. Then I burst into tears and threw myself on Martin's chest.

13

The whole of the last few weeks of anxiety and weirdness ended as I dried my eyes. It was ridiculously female of me to cry like that, and I hated it, but I had been unable to help myself.

'Maybe it's the scratch,' I said, trying to find any excuse for my weakness.

I was worried about Pepper, and that was the truth. There was no way around it.

'Come on,' said Martin. 'I had better move the airship from the graveyard before someone complains.'

We did a final sweep of the church, but found nothing. Outside, I checked on Father Thomas. He was still alive. I stayed with him while Martin went in search of a Hansom. When he came back, he and the driver lifted Thomas between them and carried him down the pathway to the cab.

I noticed the man glancing at the broken Michael-gargoyle, but he discretely said nothing.

I climbed into the cab with Thomas, leaving Martin behind to take the airship back to Long Island.

'What about the Michael-gargoyle?' I said.

'I'll take care of it,' he said.

The day had dawned, the vampires had vanished, and now there was nothing we could do until they revealed themselves again in the evening. I could only hope that Pepper was still alive and that he would remain so until we found him.

At the Church of Saint Michael and Saint Frances, Father Simon took charge of Thomas with barely a raised eyebrow at my male apparel, and I left him and the nurse to return the old man to his room. What was going to happen to him then I just didn't know. But I warned them to be vigilant and to make sure he didn't get out again that night. I didn't tell them that this would be a time of final showdown, and that it would be dangerous for us and for Thomas if he were to get in the way again.

I gave the cab driver my home address and settled back in my seat, exhaustion and anxiety making my limbs and body quiver. I felt weak, weaker than I'd ever been, and I hoped that I hadn't failed Pepper, because I knew that he would never have given up on me.

It was around 7 am by the time I crawled, fully clothed, into my bed.

I was just falling asleep when Holly jumped up on the bed beside me. She snuggled down on my pillow. My eyes flickered open. She purred, and the sound was as soothing as a lullaby. I felt her licking my hand, and the throbbing scratch stopped hurting.

I had no will left to keep my eyes open, and I fell into a dreamless sleep.

I was in the bath, soaking away all my aches and pains, when Mother and Sally finally appeared. I had managed to have four or five hours of good-quality sleep, and had felt fresher and stronger when I woke.

Mother was making a great deal of fuss as the carriage driver brought the cases in. I got out of the bath, dried and dressed in a simple day dress of pale blue. Then I went downstairs to face the expected onslaught of angry questions.

Much to my surprise, Mother merely kissed me on the cheek as I came into the kitchen. She said nothing at all as she began to make food for us all.

'I'm going to play with Holly,' Sally said. She then went off to the back yard, where I hear her chattering to the cat as if Holly understood every word she said.

'Are you all right?' Mother said.

'Yes,' I said.

'Is Mr Pepper all right too?'

I realised then that she was enquiring if I had managed to save Pepper in a way that didn't explicitly ask the question.

'He's still missing,' I said. I was tired of pretending, of trying to hide from her who I really was. 'Martin and I will try again this afternoon. Mother, I don't know how much Henry told you ...'

'I know enough. Do what you have to do, Kat. Let's just keep all of this from Sally.'

Mother and I had always been at odds over my peculiar secret life, even though she had rarely spoken out about it. Now I saw her understanding, and realised that she was coming to terms with something that she couldn't change. Maybe she was also accepting that this was something I couldn't alter either. Since those awful few days spent defending my life and that of others in Tiffany's, I had never been truly free of the darkness. It had changed me. My eyes had been opened to another world that I really couldn't just ignore anymore. I knew that if I did, it wouldn't be just my life that was at risk. It would mean the deaths of so many other innocent people as well. Perhaps even danger for Mother and Sally too. Whereas, if I kept fighting, I had a chance of keeping those I loved safe.

I wasn't arrogant enough to believe I did this alone, though. If it wasn't for Pepper and Martin, the task would have been impossible. I had to admit, though, that I loved the adventure of it all. I couldn't stop now, even if I really wanted to. Too much was at stake.

As the afternoon drew to a close, I changed back into my breeches, tied back my hair, strapped on my crossbow, stowed my knife and twisted the engagement ring around on my finger for good measure. Now I had Mother's final approval, I didn't think it necessary to hide who I was anymore. So I walked boldly out of the house and hailed a cab as if it were the most normal thing in the world for a lady to be dressed as a man.

It was still light when I met up with Martin at Saint Michael's. I noted that the broken gargoyle had gone, but didn't ask Martin how he had disposed of it. It barely seemed necessary. I knew already that the only way to completely finish one of those things was to burn it.

Martin was wearing his flame machine, which had been freshly filled with gas. But he was also sporting a crossbow with gold-tipped arrows. His was not a miniature like mine, but full size, and the arrows were longer. He was also wearing his tool-belt, which contained any tools that we might need. That night he had come as prepared as he could.

He gave me a new canister of gold-tipped arrows for my own crossbow, and I attached and loaded the mechanism ready for use.

Martin again pulled on a pair of long leather gloves to protect his hands and wrists from the potentially lethal scratches of the women.

'Two down, six to go,' I said as we entered the church.

Then we halted. The altar had been set. Two tall candles burned at either end, and a white cloth lay between them. Martin looked at me and I shrugged. Perhaps Father Thomas had escaped after all. He seemed to be very good at doing that, and I wasn't sure that the nurse or Father Simon could ever actually stop him if he, or the demon that drove him, was determined.

We moved into the chapel cautiously. Martin scanned from side to side on the left, while I mimicked him on the right. We both held our crossbows. The shadows remained clear. None of the vampires was there, and neither was Pepper.

As we reached the altar, the door to the vestry creaked open. A cool breeze wafted through the chapel and blew out the nearest candle. It didn't make much difference to the level of light, fortunately.

I found myself face to face with Father Simon.

'What are you doing here?' he asked.

'We're looking for my friend, George Pepper. The creatures took him last night.'

Simon seemed confused. 'Creatures? What creatures?'

'The vampires that marked Father Thomas and killed Father Michael and Father Anthony,' I said. 'Father, you should leave here, it isn't safe for you.'

Father Simon's eyes glazed over and a twisted smile moved his mouth as though some cruel puppeteer had threaded string through his lips.

'Oh no. Not you too,' Martin said.

Father Simon advanced on us with his arms outstretched in an obscene parody of the crucifixion. I stepped back and almost fell over the destroyed Jesus figure. The irony was not lost on me.

Martin raised his crossbow and aimed it at the priest.

'You can't *kill* him!' I said. 'He may be salvageable if we destroy *her*.'

'They are relying on our refusal to kill an innocent person. They are trying to distract us. Don't you see that, Kat?'

'I know. But how can we avoid it?'

Simon dived at Martin, and I ducked under his outstretched arms and ran toward the vestry. There I saw what I should have seen the day before – and I cursed under my breath at my stupidity. The worn rug we had ignored was now turned up, and underneath it I could see a groove cut into the floor. There was a trapdoor!

'Martin, keep him busy, I've found something.'

I heard Martin and the priest grapple as I pushed the rug aside. Beneath it, as I suspected, was a broad, heavy trapdoor with a thick metal ring-pull. I tried to lift it, but it was heavier than I had expected, and I looked around for something that could be used to lever it up. The room was bare, and I placed my hand on my hips in consternation. My fingers touched the Remington, and I realised that this was the answer. I pulled it free from its holster and, placing the barrel in the ring, used it to haul the trapdoor up.

Once I could get my hands underneath, I began to heave, but the weight was too much.

I heard a loud thump and glanced toward the chapel. Martin had knocked Father Simon down. The priest wasn't moving. The heavy trapdoor slipped and fell back into place with a crash. Talk about enough to wake the dead! I feared that Martin had killed Simon, but was glad when he joined me in the vestry.

'Help me with this,' I said.

I took another glance over to the chapel. Simon lay still beneath the altar. I saw a trickle of blood seeping from his head into the grooves between the flagstones. I closed my eyes, then turned away. I used my Remington once more to start lifting the trap door. Martin caught hold of the heavy wood, and the two of us managed to push the door back until it flopped into an open position, tilting back from the dark aperture.

No mere human could have lifted the trapdoor alone, which made it obvious to me that this must be somewhere that was being used by the vampires.

The fading light seeped into the hole. I could make out a set of steep stone steps leading down into some kind of basement. The steps looked worn and well-used, and they led to goodness knew where.

I was beginning to wish we had arrived sooner. It occurred to me that the sensible thing to do would be to return in the morning, when full daylight would be our companion. Unfortunately, though, we didn't have any choice but to proceed, if we were to have any hope at all of saving Pepper's life.

'It's probably a catacomb,' Martin said. 'Or an underground crypt.'

'It wasn't on the church plans,' I noted.

'Charles Addams must have had two sets of

plans. This couldn't have been built after the church was erected.'

'Hmm. So what was his agenda?' I wondered.

Martin brought the remaining lit candle from the altar.

'Don't tell me you didn't think to bring some safer form of lighting?' I said.

'I'm not perfect, Kat,' he said.

He sounded wounded, and I quickly apologised for my rudeness. It was obvious that Martin was just as worried about Pepper as I was. In those circumstances anyone could make mistakes.

The stairs wound downwards, and I found myself counting them as we descended into the damp, dark, musty bowels of the church. There were over a hundred steps, and I was glad for the small amount of light that the candle afforded us, since there was no way that natural daylight could find its way down there.

When we finally reached the bottom, we found ourselves in a small open area with numerous arched passageways leading off. The arches were in the same architectural style as used above. I was certain that Charles Addams had certainly designed this. Even if these chambers had been added at a later time, this simple element confirmed that he had been very much involved. Though how and why, we didn't know.

'Which way?' I whispered. I was very much aware that our vampire enemies would be down there somewhere, and although I wanted to confront them, I didn't want them to know we were there until we were in a position to take them on and win. I hoped they hadn't heard the crash as the trapdoor had slammed shut when I first tried to raise it.

Martin drew closer to the nearest arch and raised

the candle. We studied the markings above the arch, then moved onto the next.

There were nine openings in all.

'This one,' Martin said finally.

'Why? Is it different from the rest?'

'No. We just have to start somewhere.'

I couldn't argue with his reasoning, since there was no way of working out logically which one to take. So I followed him as he began to hurry down the passage. It was lined with recessed areas, which were full of cobwebbed rubble. Some of them had ancient stone coffins in them, and one or two contained a jumble of bones. Unfortunately luck was not on our side, as the passage terminated in a dead end.

'That rules this one out then,' I said, and turned back.

The next three either ended in similar dead ends or else slowly diminished in height until they became impassable.

'This is the one,' Martin said as we made our way down the fifth tunnel. I had no idea why he thought that, but after a few yards the passage opened up into a large cavern.

I was overwhelmed as we moved into this space. It stretched high up, like a natural underground cave. The walls were punctuated with what looked like fissures, but there was no apparent way of getting up there and into them.

'We can't still be directly underneath the church,' I observed.

'Unlikely given the distance we have just walked. This place is under something else entirely.'

'What do you think it is?'

'My guess is, that's their resting place,' Martin

whispered. 'It couldn't be any safer. We have no hope at all of getting up there to catch them as they sleep. Unless ...'

He fumbled with his tool-belt but couldn't find whatever gadget he was looking for.

'It may well be,' he continued, 'the reason why the church was built where it is. Perhaps this place has always been here?'

'Possible,' I turned around, counting the holes. 'Nine. Unless I'm mistaken.'

Martin checked. 'No, you're right.'

'That means there is one of them here that we haven't seen,' I said, my hushed voice echoing around the space.

'So, two down, seven to go then,' Martin said. 'I don't think we are prepared enough.'

It wasn't like Martin to be so negative, but I knew what he meant. The whole thing was more overwhelming than anything we had faced before, and I understood why. Our friend's life was in jeopardy. We couldn't give up, even if our own lives were at stake.

I was at a loss as to how to proceed. This was a strange situation. We had no way of sneaking up on the vampires, and if we disturbed them it would bring them all out in force in one go. I wasn't sure we could deal with them all at once.

'There may be another way up,' Martin said. 'We haven't tried all of the tunnels.'

'True. It's also possible that Pepper isn't up there with them. Maybe we can find him while they sleep. If he's still okay, we can get him out of here and pick our battle on another day,' I suggested.

The cavern was empty but for the openings, and there was no sign at all of Pepper. The idea that he could be in one of the other tunnels wasn't a far-fetched notion. Anything was possible, and it was worth exploring further before we returned to the airship for climbing equipment that could help us scale the wall and explore the caves above.

I had nothing else to offer, so we turned and left as quietly as we had entered.

The sixth passage came to a dead end, as did the seventh and eighth, but the ninth proved far more interesting. At its end, it opened out into a smaller grotto. Ahead of us was a pair of closed, wrought iron gates. Martin raised the candle higher so that the light would cast out farther. This was an underground crypt in which were nine stone sarcophaguses.

'I think we've found our vampires after all,' I said. Could it be that easy?

The gates weren't locked but were poorly maintained, and they squeaked as I pushed against them.

In each corner of the tomb someone had placed a small fire drum complete with oil and kindling. Martin held the candle to the kindling in each drum, and they all slowly guttered into flame. The room filled with light – relieving us our reliance on the candle – and slowly started to warm up.

'That makes me feel a whole lot more secure,' I whispered as Martin came to my side. 'But it all seems a trifle too convenient.'

Martin blew out the candle and stowed it in his spare arrow cartridge. 'No point in wasting it until we need to see to get back up the stairs.'

I was anxious to proceed with our investigation, as time was moving on. It could have been an illusion, brought on by being so far underground, but I was sure the last of the afternoon was rapidly giving way to the evening above ground, meaning that our enemy would rise soon.

Martin pulled a crowbar out of his tool belt and we began to lever off the lid of the nearest sarcophagus. Light from the drums flickered on the stone walls, casting moving shadows that had me constantly looking around.

The lid shifted with a loud stone-on-stone scraping sound, and the pair of us froze, almost expecting vampires to leap at us from every corner.

Inside the first coffin Serena lay asleep. She looked as serene as her name suggested, and beautiful too. She was still wearing the strange black leather clothing, and her short, shoulder-length black hair was groomed and shiny.

Martin pressed his loaded crossbow against Serena's chest. He fired, and the arrow powered silently through her. Her eyes opened and grew wide, her lips parted in a silent cry and her whole body stiffened. I saw one sharp fang protrude as though she were a cat that had lost one of its main teeth. It was on the right side of her mouth, and it looked odd and imbalanced. Then she died, rapidly consumed in a tracery of red fire that turned her into nothing more than a pile of rust–coloured dust.

Martin pulled the arrow back out of the pile of ashes and replaced it in his canister. The tip was dented from its impact with the bottom of the sepulchre, but it would serve again.

The next sarcophagus was empty. In the third we found Pepper. His eyes were open and he appeared to be in something of a catatonic state. Keen to free him, I hefted the lid away. I wanted him out of there as quickly as possible. The lid teetered on the edge, then toppled, falling down with a loud crash onto the floor.

'Get him out of here,' I said. 'I'll finish what we started.'

'No,' said Martin. '*We* will finish it. Pepper isn't in any immediate danger.'

'As long as he doesn't gargoyle on us,' I said.

We left our friend, and I helped Martin push aside the lids of two more sarcophaguses. One was empty, the other revealed Mortice inside. I finished her off quickly. This time I used my golden blade to cut her throat. As she died, she smiled at me, as though I had done her the greatest favour, or as if her death was some amusing irony.

'Four left,' Martin said. 'We need to find Lucia. If we finish her, we end them all.'

I opened the next sarcophagus, to find Marion lying within. She was breathing strangely, eyes wide open, but she didn't react to me. She was almost in the same state as Pepper, except that I noticed a green puddle of slime that seemed to pool around her shoulder. The gold from the arrow I had pierced her with was working on her, despite it having been pulled from the wound almost immediately. She was slowly dying from it. Martin ended her struggling life, while I began to push aside the lid of the next sarcophagus.

Within was Lucia, lying as calm and as beautiful as the others.

She didn't move as I slid the stone slab aside, but as I raised the gold–plated dagger she suddenly opened her eyes and threw her weight upwards, knocking me, and the heavy stone lid, back. I fell to the hard floor, hitting my already injured head and jarring my neck in the process. Yes, it appeared that 1865 was a very good year for concussion; but I knew that if I didn't get up, then Lucia would kill me. I rolled to my feet just as she climbed out of the sarcophagus and leapt with one bound to land right in front of me. I didn't hesitate; I swung the knife. It met with thin air.

The wind was knocked from me as Priscilla dived into me from behind, but I recovered quickly, rolling aside as her clawing nails ran the length of my right arm, drawing blood. I knew this was an effort to make me drop the blade, but I clung tighter to the hilt and turned around to bring it up between us. Priscilla drew back and paused. Her face glazed over as though she had slipped from our reality into another. Then, just as suddenly, she fell on me. She yelped, and as we rolled, the knife was yanked viciously from my fingers.

I was smashed painfully against one of the stone coffins. Then Priscilla rolled away, screaming her insanity and hatred. I quickly recovered my senses, pulling my bruised and battered body back off the ground. I realised that Priscilla must have fallen on the knife during our struggle, as its blade was now buried under her ribs. Her death was slow, agonising and overdramatic.

As she burst into flames and then crumbled to dust, calling once more for her beloved spike, I was left wondering where she had got that odd, English-like accent from anyway ...

Meanwhile, Martin was fending off Natasha, who had emerged from the remaining sarcophagus. She was now semi-clad in a strange top that barely covered her breasts and left her midriff exposed, and she wore an elaborate headdress that I would have found annoying but seemed not to trouble her.

I looked around for Lucia. She was making her

way out of the gates, with Pepper in her arms. He seemed to be partly conscious now, and he cast me a pleading glance that told me he was not completely lost to her demonic hypnosis. I knew that I couldn't let her get away – especially not with Pepper in tow – but was concerned about leaving Martin alone with Natasha. She appeared to be the most vicious of all of the vampires, and I didn't want my other friend to be at risk either.

'Martin, Lucia is getting away!'

'I'm all right. Go after her!' he said.

I picked my gold knife out of the dusty remains of Priscilla and freed the crossbow from my belt. Then I loaded an arrow while following Lucia out through the iron gates and down the passage.

The stairs were difficult to negotiate in the dark, and exhausting to climb, but I reached the top in time to see Lucia leading Pepper into the chapel. With her speed and agility they should have been there sooner. I couldn't help wondering if Pepper had done his best to delay her.

I had no time to pause and gain my breath. This was it. Now or never. I raised the crossbow and fired, but my shaking and exhausted fingers sent the shot wide, and the arrow buried itself in the vestry door frame.

'Damn!'

I forced myself into a second wind, pushing back the pain of my screaming lungs as I loaded the next arrow, then followed Lucia and Pepper into the chapel.

My breath ran out as I found Lucia feeding on Pepper's wrist as he lay prone over the altar.

I raised the crossbow and fired, but at that moment Father Simon came out of the shadows and yanked the bow from my hands.

'What are you doing?' I yelled. 'I'm trying to free you.'

'I don't wish to be freed,' Simon said.

I glanced at Lucia to see that she had released Pepper. He slumped to the ground. I could see he was still human, but his skin was so white it glowed like marble. He was holding onto his soul, though, with every ounce of strength left in his body.

Simon raised my crossbow, pointing it not at Lucia but at me.

'Finish him,' Simon instructed Lucia. 'I need to feed.'

'I can't,' Lucia gasped. 'His will is too strong. He hasn't lost his faith yet, master.'

The truth of the moment sank in. Simon was more than Thomas's carer, he was his controller! This was no ordinary gargoyle infection, if indeed he was a gargoyle at all.

'Who are you?' I asked. 'Only, I know you aren't really a priest.'

Simon's lips lifted in a sneer, one long fang protruding over his lip. The imbalance was far more sinister than if he had possessed a pair of the cat-like teeth. I also realised that his was on the opposite side of the mouth to the women's. The fang was a mini dagger, and it would pierce, rip and penetrate its victim just as effectively. But why just one?

'I'm no priest. I'm no gargoyle. But they all do my bidding,' boasted Simon. 'Lucia is my bride, you see, and she brought the others into the fold. There have to be nine in a vampire coven. One master, and eight females to bring home the food. Though it can be done with just the two of us.'

'You can't take the food for yourself?' I asked.

Simon sneered. 'You know nothing of our ways.'

'No, I don't. But if you're going to kill me, then at least give me the satisfaction of learning something.'

'Charles?' said Lucia. She was bending over Pepper again. 'I'll try. I'll try to do this alone.'

I suddenly realised who he was.

'You're *Charles Addams*,' I said. 'Now I understand why the church is as it is. And why you have a spell carved into the eves. This was some awful scheme you hatched, even at the planning stage.'

'You are very intelligent. I see, also, that one of the girls has given you *my* mark?' Addams said.

'Mark?' I was confused for a moment, then I remembered the scratch on the back of my hand.

'Thanks to you, I will now need to replenish my ranks ...'

'Sorry, Charles, but I'm just not interested in joining your little family.'

'It might be enough,' Lucia said. 'She's the thing he holds onto. Bring her in, Charles.'

'I said no.'

'You don't have a choice. You're already becoming one of us,' Charles said.

'Oh, but I do,' I insisted.

I threw the knife that I had been hiding behind my back, and it landed with practised precision right in Lucia's throat.

Lucia made a hideous gurgling noise and clutched ineffectually at her throat as the gold began to glow inside her. Then she burst into rivulets of flame, falling against the altar, where the white cloth caught and the fire spread up the fabric and over the stone.

Addams screamed: an ear-splitting noise that

wasn't unlike the cry of a wolf, only amplified many times over. I had killed his bride. He had every right to be furious. And if what he had said was true, he now couldn't feed.

I threw myself out of his line of fire and dived toward the altar, where I caught hold of Pepper and began to pull him away from the flames.

Addams was enraged. I guess that happens when a species of monster realises it is about to become extinct. He fired the crossbow, and an arrow whipped past my head and ricocheted off the altar.

I continued to pull Pepper away from the flames, taking shelter behind one of the upturned pews. Then, something very strange occurred. I felt a sharpness in my tooth, and one long, thin fang pushed down and over my lip from the right side of my mouth. I looked at Pepper and felt a sudden pang of hunger. He was not my friend. He was food.

Behind me, Addams laughed.

14

Pepper was ridiculously attractive to me once more. The magnetism was ten times what it had been before. His blue eyes appeared bluer than the sea, his pale skin as flawless as a renaissance angel and his blond hair so pale and shiny that I could imagine seeing my reflection in it.

'Not you ... Kat,' he said, staring up at me.

A tear rolled down his cheek. I stared at it as though it were the most beautiful thing I have ever seen. Then my fascination caused me to follow the silver stain back to his eye.

I saw my own image in his dilated pupil. I didn't like what I saw. Black flame swirled in my eyes. The hideous single fang was dripping with a poisonous saliva. I drew back from Pepper, appalled by myself.

'No ... Pepper ... this can't be me.'

But it was. I had become the thing that I was hunting.

Addams began to exert his master control over me. I felt in my mind the tug and pull to obey him without question. He wanted me to drain Pepper of his blood and soul. But with the vampiric connection, all of my unanswered questions were now clear in my head. I could read Charles. I knew how he had fooled me.

It was so easy: I had not thought him a demon, because he had been working at the church and I had seen him in daylight. Those two things combined had made him above my suspicion. But the truth was, he hadn't been the Father Simon I had witnessed talking to Paddy at all. He had only *appeared* to be.

Somehow, when Pepper and Martin had left the church after our first visit, I had lapsed into a fugue. Already the power of the demon had stretched out and touched me: just by entering the church, we had allowed him to see us, and then his magic had helped him to focus on our attempts to learn the truth.

When I had woken in Saint Michael and Saint Frances' church, I had imagined I had been awake throughout the Mass. I had believed that Simon had led it. Maybe the real Father Simon had.

Then, when Charles had got me firmly under this confusing spell, he had taken me from the church, not in daylight as I had believed, but in darkness.

Father Jonas's home was genuine. There Charles had clouded both my mind and the nurse's. He had allowed Thomas to tell me his story, then had forced me to completely forget it.

It was all a game to him, you see. He and his women loved to amuse themselves by bringing misery on humans, even when they weren't feeding off them. Why he hadn't killed me instead was the only mystery that remained unsolved.

Afterwards it had been he who had led me to Saint Michael's, and I realised that Father Thomas must have followed us. By sheer willpower he had tried to help me. I just hadn't seen the warning signs.

I was plummeted out of my mind connection with Addams as he began to yelp. Pepper was cradling me.

'You were having some kind of seizure,' he said.

I shook my head to try to clear it. I was free of Addams' control. Now was the time to act. I sat up and saw my cat, Holly, inexplicably clinging to Addams' head. Her long, sharp claws were buried into his scalp, and no matter how hard he shook himself or tried to pull her away, he could not dislodge her.

The flames around the altar were dying down now that the cloth had burnt through and there was nothing but stone to feed on. Pepper slumped as though the last bit of strength he had was fading. I had to do something. I rolled back toward the ashes of Lucia and searched for my knife, but as my hand reached for the blade I felt an unreasonable fear and revulsion. The gold ring on my finger began to burn and glow.

'This can't be happening!' I cried. I yanked the ring from my finger, tossing it to the ground as my fingers blistered at its touch.

Time was running out, and if I didn't do something soon, I would become Addams's pawn again – this time, permanently. I could delay no longer.

I grabbed the knife by the hilt, which fortunately was not made of gold. Then I stood up and ran at the screaming vampire as my cat continued to claw and distract him.

An arrow burst from the crossbow still clutched in Addams' hand, and I ducked aside as it whistled past me, knowing that the gold tips were now as lethal to me as they had been to the vampires. I reached Addams just as he managed to dislodge Holly. Or maybe Holly had chosen her moment well. Who knew with that cat? She was as mysterious to me then as she had been when I first found her.

I fell on Addams, but he was as solid as stone, and even though I could feel new vampiric strength pumping into my muscles, I was no match for him. As I tried to bring the knife up between us, he twisted my wrist and forced it from my fingers. I yelped in pain and frustration. I pulled back, then delivered a kick to Addams' fingers, sending the crossbow careering diagonally over the chapel's stone floor.

I threw myself back on the man. We fell to the floor and rolled as I hit and punched him with as much strength as I could muster. I had never hated anyone so much. Nor had I been more vicious. Unfortunately, Addams controlled the roll we were in, and ended up on top of me. I was pinned down.

'Time to complete your transformation, Miss Lightfoot,' Addams said. 'I will enjoy using you as my slave.'

I didn't like the sound of that, nor the sight of the long fang as it grew once more over his lip. This close, I could see it was hollow, and dripping with some kind of toxin. He reminded me of a snake about to deliver a dose of deadly venom.

I bucked beneath him, but to no avail. Where was that cat when you really needed her?

Addams laughed, then bent his head. I arched away, trying to make it as difficult as possible for the monster to bite me.

Then, as Addams was about to strike, I saw Pepper towering over us. He had my knife in his hand.

My eyes widened. I was willing him to strike, and I watched in slow motion as his arm came down.

He buried the knife in Addams' back.

Addams gasped. The strength ran out of his body, and I was able to push him aside before the flame tracers ignited from the gold.

He fell back on the knife, pushing the blade farther in, and I dragged my shaking limbs up from the ground by gripping one of the pews.

Then, taking Pepper's hand, I pulled him away from the heat. We watched Addams burn and disintegrate to dust.

As Addams fell to ashes, Martin joined us. He was covered in blood, and I knew that Natasha had died hard at his hands also. But I could tell by the look on his face that this battle had taken its toll on him. I don't think any of us had ever before been so exhausted.

Pepper stood like a statue beside me until I turned to him and placed my arms around him, while pulling Martin into our joint embrace.

'That was something else,' I said when the trembling stopped and I was able to speak. There was so much emotion coursing through me, and the adrenaline crash had happened far quicker than usual.

I checked Pepper over, and he appeared to be his normal self, even though he was a little subdued. I, however, felt anything but normal.

'I don't feel right,' I said. 'Help me find my blade in that mess.'

Martin searched for the blade in the ashes as I looked around the chapel.

'This place needs to burn,' he said. 'While there is still that spell up in the eves, it will be a magnet to the likes of Addams. We don't need another coven moving in.'

'Holly?' I called. 'Where is that cat?'

'Cat?' asked Martin.

'Yes, Holly was here. If it hadn't been for her ...'

But the cat was nowhere to be found.

We picked up our weapons, and Martin and Pepper went around the chapel beams and placed charges with sticks of dynamite on them. For good measure, Martin lit his flame machine and began a fire by igniting the damaged pews. We left the church.

Outside I fell to my knees. Something wasn't right. I felt a compulsion to return to the chapel, and I would have gone back inside if Pepper and Martin hadn't helped me stay back.

'What's wrong with her?' asked Pepper.

Martin pulled me onto the street and under one of the gaslights. He pulled back my lips and checked my teeth, then looked deeply into my eyes.

'Oh no,' he said.

'What is it?' I asked.

'You're a semi-vampire.'

'What in the name of all that is gracious is a semi-vampire?' Pepper said.

'Well, it's sort of vampire, but only half turned,' Martin explained.

'That's not possible,' I protested. 'We killed Addams. I should have reverted back to my former self.'

'What rule book said that?' Martin asked. 'I'm sorry, but that is the way things are.'

'Am I ... going to *bite* people?' I asked.

Martin was silent for a moment. 'I don't know.'

'Am I still allergic to gold?'

Martin pulled my engagement ring from his

pocket. 'I found this on the floor inside.'

I reached out to touch it. I didn't feel the same revulsion I had inside the church, but that didn't mean it wouldn't burn me. I touched one finger to the gold. It didn't start to glow, and it didn't burn.

'Phew,' I said.

I took the ring from Martin's hand and was about to place it in my pocket when the first stick of dynamite ignited. The ground shook beneath us.

'Let's get out of here before someone calls the cops,' said Martin.

We crossed to the other side of the street, then ducked into an alley to watch. The church burned ferociously, the roof beams crashing down into the ruins, and after no time at all it was a bonfire of burning wood. At one point I thought I saw Holly moving in the shadows of a fire escape above our head.

'Did you see that?' I asked.

'What?' asked Pepper.

I glanced up once more. The fire escape was empty. There was no sign of the cat.

'Never mind,' I said.

Holly looked up at me as I opened Sally's bedroom door and looked in. The cat was curled up at the bottom of the bed as she always was. The light from the hallway illuminated her eyes, which glowed green.

'One of these days I'm going to learn your secret,' I whispered.

And damn but that cat actually winked at me.

She settled back down to sleep as I backed away and closed the door.

I meant what I had said. One day I would

understand who and what she was, but how or when that would happen I didn't know.

Downstairs, Mother was waiting. She gave me a glass of red wine that looked like blood – more irony – and I sat down with her in the lounge. All was quiet, and I sipped the wine. The alcohol helped to calm my nerves. How was I going to tell her that the night's events had changed me, possibly forever?

We sat in silence. There seemed no need to speak. It was enough for her that I had returned safely and the task of saving Pepper was done.

Epilogue

Father Thomas's funeral was something of a stately affair. The old man had died peacefully in his sleep the night after we brought down Saint Michael's church. I had seen him before those final moments, however, and I knew that there was no longer any need for his remains to be burnt. The demon had left him; the spell, now that Addams was dead, was completely broken.

As Pepper, Martin and I sat in the rear pew, I looked around the church. Part of me expected to see Lucia in her dark veil, but all I saw was a group of normal people who had come together to celebrate the life of a man whom they had looked up to.

'Tanks fer everting,' Paddy said, nodding to us as he passed.

He looked better. For one thing, he was completely sober; for another, his clothing was washed and pressed and his hair was groomed and slicked back neatly from his face. He was with a woman and a young girl, whom Pepper recognised as Paddy's landlady, Paula, and her daughter, Romy. They looked like the makings of a family.

Later we moved outside to the churchyard, and as

Thomas's body was being lowered into the ground, I squinted up at the autumn sky. The daylight didn't exactly hurt me, but I didn't feel too comfortable in it anymore.

I glanced around the churchyard. From beside one of the gravestones, Holly was watching me. I touched the fang scar on the back of my hand. I remembered the cat licking the wound. I remembered feeling it heal. But I didn't know what that meant at all.

After the funeral, the three of us walked back to King George's Tavern, where we had first discussed the mystery of Saint Michael's church. We took up residence in the back room again. Every good team needs a base in which to discuss strategy, and this place was as good as any.

While Martin went to fetch us drinks, I placed the engagement ring on the table in front of Pepper.

'Pepper, you know that we … You know it was just the vampire's spell … right?'

He scooped up the ring, placing it quickly in the pocket that held his watch.

'I'll keep it for you,' he said, and smiled.

Then I knew that for Pepper there had never been a spell to make him love me. The truth was, the thing between us had begun long before they had contaminated him. I just wasn't ready to admit it. Nor to commit to a permanent future under the current circumstances.

Rejecting him like that made me feel awful, but I couldn't change the way things were. The truth was that I was more dangerous to him now than those awful women had been. I didn't know what was going to happen in my strange part-vampire state, nor if I could be trusted ever to be alone with a man again.

There was no hunger, there was no allergy, and when I scrutinised my eyes in the mirror, I never saw that black flame lurking in the back of them. I could see better in the dark than I ever had before. Even so, I didn't feel as though I was a demon, and my urge to destroy them was stronger than ever. When I bared my teeth, there were two, not one, of the fang tips just showing at the top of my canines. I had no idea how or when the fangs might emerge, and hoped that I could control it when the time came. This anomaly didn't inspire me with confidence though.

'I need to figure some things out,' I said, because I wanted to explain.

'I know,' Pepper answered.

Martin returned with our drinks, we smiled at each other and drank together, and just like that, things were back to normal with the three of us.

Well – as normal as they could be, anyway.

About The Author

Award winning author Sam Stone began her professional writing career in 2007 when her first novel won the Silver Award for Best Novel with *ForeWord Magazine* Book of the Year Awards. Since then she has gone on to write several novels, three novellas and many short stories. She was the first woman in 31 years to win the British Fantasy Society Award for Best Novel. She also won the award for Best Short Fiction in the same year (2011).

Stone loves all genus fiction and enjoys mixing horror (her first passion) with a variety of different genres including science fiction, fantasy and steampunk.

Her works can be found in paperback, audio and e-book.

More Titles By Sam Stone

With Telos Publishing

KAT LIGHTFOOT MYSTERIES
Steampunk, horror, adventure series
1: ZOMBIES AT TIFFANY'S (Aug 2012)
2: KAT ON A HOT TIN AIRSHIP (Aug 2013)
3: WHAT'S DEAD PUSSYKAT (Sept 2014)
4: KAT OF GREEN TENTACLES (Coming in 2015)

JINX CHRONICLES
Hi-tech science fiction fantasy series
1: JINX TOWN (Nov 2014)
2: JINX MAGIC (Sept 2015)
3: JINX BOUND (Sept 2016)

THE DARKNESS WITHIN (Feb 2014)
Science Fiction Horror Short Novel

ZOMBIES IN NEW YORK AND OTHER BLOODY
JOTTINGS (Feb 2011)
Thirteen stories of horror and passion, and six mythological
and erotic poems from the pen of the new Queen of Vampire
fiction.

Other Titles

THE VAMPIRE GENE SERIES
Horror, thriller, time-travel series.
1: KILLING KISS (Sep 2008)
2: FUTILE FLAME (Sep 2009)
3: DEMON DANCE (Sep 2010)
4: HATEFUL HEART (Sep 2011)
5: SILENT SAND (Sep 2012)
6: JADED JEWEL (coming in 2015)

SAM STONE

ZOMBIES AT TIFFANY'S

ZOMBIES AT TIFFANY'S
Kat Lightfoot Mysteries #1

Kat Lightfoot thought that getting a job at the famed Tiffany's store in New York would be the end to her problems ... She has money, new friends, and there's even an inventor working there who develops new weapons from clockwork, and who cuts diamonds with a strange powered light. This is 1862, after all, and such things are the wonder of the age.

But then events take a turn for the worse: men and women wander the streets talking of 'the darkness'; bodies vanish from morgues across town; and random, bloody attacks on innocent people take place in broad daylight.

Soon Kat and her friends are fighting for their lives against a horde of infected people, with only their wits and ingenuity to help them.

A steampunked story of diamonds, chutzpah, death and horror from the blood-drenched pen of Sam Stone.

ISBN: 978-1-84583-072-4
RRP £9.99

'SAM STONE ROCKS!' ROBERT RANKIN
SAM STONE
KAT ON A HOT TIN AIRSHIP

KAT ON A HOT TIN AIRSHIP
Kat Lightfoot Mysteries #2

It is 1865 and the American Civil War has come to an end. Now Kat Lightfoot finds herself in the middle of another kind of war: a family feud involving her brother Henry and his new wife. But what is behind the strange behaviour of this affluent Southern family?

Caught in the crossfire of an implacable spirit's attempt to wreak vengeance on the Pollitt family, Kat must once again enlist the help of journalist George Pepper and the inventor Martin Crewe to find out what really haunts the family's past.

In order to learn what devastating secrets the Pollitts are hiding she must first explore her own feelings for Maggie's brother Orlando, who is one of the seductive Nephilim.

A ghostly steampunked tale of family secrets, voodoo and vengeance from the author of *Zombies at Tiffany's* – to which this book is a sequel.

ISBN: 978-1-84583-086-1
RRP £12.99

THE DARKNESS WITHIN
Final Cut

Chief Engineer Madison Whitehawk suspects foul play when a series of small anomalies occur aboard the ark ship Freedom. But Madison's fears are nothing compared to the impending disaster heading their way.

As the team of scientists, engineers and crew take their precious cargo of colonists towards New Earth a deadly parasite has found its way onboard.

Soon Madison, Second Officer Crichton and colonist Syra Connor are fighting for their lives against trusted friends and former lovers.

What is the parasite that changes the minds and behaviour of those it infects? And how can the crew of the Freedom destroy the darkness within?

A thrilling sci-fi/horror novel from award-winning author Sam Stone.

ISBN: 978-1-84583-874-4
RRP £10.99

ZOMBIES IN NEW YORK
AND OTHER BLOODY JOTTINGS

SAM STONE

FOREWORD BY GRAHAM MASTERTON

ZOMBIES IN NEW YORK
& Other Bloody Jottings

Something is sapping the energy of the usually robust dancers of the Moulin Rouge ... Zombies roam the streets of New York City ... Clowns die in mysteriously humorous ways ... Jack the Ripper's crimes are investigated by a vampire ...

Welcome to the horrific and poetic world of Sam Stone, where angels are stalking the undead and a vampire becomes obsessed with a centuries-old werewolf. Terror and lust go hand in hand in the disturbing world of the Toymaker, and the haunting Siren's call draws the hapless further into a waking nightmare.

Thirteen stories of horror and passion, and six mythological and erotic poems from the new queen of vampire fiction.

Chick-slash has never been so entertaining

Contains the 2011 British Fantasy Award Winning short story 'Fool's Gold'.

ISBN: 978-1-84583-864-5
RRP £12.99

OTHER TELOS TITLES

HORROR/FANTASY

GRAHAM MASTERTON
THE DJINN
RULES OF DUEL (With William S Burroughs)

SIMON CLARK
HUMPTY'S BONES
THE FALL

DAVID J HOWE
TALESPINNING
Horror collection of stories, extracts and screenplays

URBAN GOTHIC: LACUNA AND OTHER TRIPS edited by
DAVID J HOWE
Tales of horror from and inspired by the *Urban Gothic*
television series. Contributors: Graham Masterton,
Christopher Fowler, Simon Clark, Steve Lockley & Paul
Lewis, Paul Finch and Debbie Bennett.

RAVEN DANE
ABSINTHE & ARSENIC
16 tales of Victorian horror, Steampunk adventures and dark,
deadly, obsession
DEATH'S DARK WINGS (Coming in 2015)
Exciting alternative history with a supernatural twist

CAPTAINS STUPENDOUS by RHYS HUGHES
Steampunk humorous adventure about the Fantastical
Faraway Brothers

SPECTRE by STEPHEN LAWS
Something is stalking the Chapter, picking them off one by one, something connected with their past, and with the girl they used to know.

BREATHE by CHRISTOPHER FOWLER
The Office meets *Night of the Living Dead*.

KIT COX
DOCTOR TRIPPS SERIES
A Neo-Victorian world where steam is pitted against diesel, but which side will win?
KAIJU COCKTAIL
MOON MONSTER (coming in 2015)

KING OF ALL THE DEAD by STEVE LOCKLEY & PAUL LEWIS
The king of all the dead will have what is his.

THE HUMAN ABSTRACT by GEORGE MANN
A future tale of private detectives, AIs, Nanobots, love and death.

HOUDINI'S LAST ILLUSION by STEVE SAVILE
Can the master illusionist Harry Houdini outwit the dead shades of his past?

ALICE'S JOURNEY BEYOND THE MOON by R J CARTER
A sequel to the classic Lewis Carroll tales.

APPROACHING OMEGA by ERIC BROWN
A colonisation mission to Earth runs into problems.

VALLEY OF LIGHTS by STEPHEN GALLAGHER
A cop comes up against a body-hopping murderer.

PRETTY YOUNG THINGS by DOMINIC McDONAGH
A nest of lesbian rave bunny vampires is at large in Manchester.

A MANHATTAN GHOST STORY by T M WRIGHT
Do you see ghosts? A classic tale of love and the supernatural.

BLACK TIDE by DEL STONE JR
A college professor and his students find themselves trapped by an encroaching horde of zombies following a waste spillage.

FORCE MAJEURE by DANIEL O'MAHONY
An incredible fantasy novel.

SHROUDED BY DARKNESS: TALES OF TERROR edited by ALISON L R DAVIES
An anthology of tales guaranteed to bring a chill to the spine. This collection has been published to raise money for DebRA. Featuring stories by: Debbie Bennett, Poppy Z Brite, Simon Clark, Storm Constantine, Peter Crowther, Alison L R Davies, Paul Finch, Christopher Fowler, Neil Gaiman, Gary Greenwood, David J Howe, Dawn Knox, Tim Lebbon, Charles de Lint, Steven Lockley & Paul Lewis, James Lovegrove, Graham Masterton, Richard Christian Matheson, Justina Robson, Mark Samuels, Darren Shan and Michael Marshall Smith. With a frontispiece by Clive Barker and a foreword by Stephen Jones. Deluxe hardback cover by Simon Marsden.

CRIME

ANDREW HOOK
A series of exciting crime novels putting a neo–noir twist on the genre conventions of bums and dames
THE IMMORTALISTS
CHURCH OF WIRE (Coming 2015)

PRISCILLA MASTERS
Titles in Priscilla Masters' acclaimed Joanna Piercy series
1. WINDING UP THE SERPENT
2. CATCH THE FALLING SPARROW
3. A WREATH FOR MY SISTER
4. AND NONE SHALL SLEEP
5. EMBROIDERING SHROUDS
6. SCARING CROWS

MIKE RIPLEY
Fitzroy Maclean Angel Series
JUST ANOTHER ANGEL
ANGEL TOUCH
ANGEL HUNT
ANGEL ON THE INSIDE
ANGEL CONFIDENTIAL
ANGEL CITY
ANGELS IN ARMS
FAMILY OF ANGELS
BOOTLEGGED ANGEL
THAT ANGEL LOOK
LIGHTS, CAMERA, ANGEL
ANGEL UNDERGROUND